The lush marshy land of Brazoria stretched as far as I could see. Some twenty miles southeast lay the smoggy halo of ancient Houston with its priceless historical district, the only extensive group of pre-twenty-first century buildings north of Old Mexico.

Here, right at the edge of the spaceport, was the verdant, feverish border of the Brazoria Republic of Texas, one hundred years in the dust of history. Here the North American Madness hordes had been held back by Texans fighting beside an odd lot of computers, AI robots, alpha-chimpanzees, and "machine-lover anti-humanists" who had escaped from the north. There was a pyramid monument nearby, another half a kilometer west, another beyond that; and the same to the east. A line of memorials to the battles of the Madness . . .

The one near me marked the spot where the last anthropoid ape had been killed.

JUSTIN LEIBER

BEYOND HUMANITY

A TOM DOHERTY ASSOCIATES BOOK

BEYOND HUMANITY

Copyright © 1987 by Justin Leiber

All rights reserved, including the right to reproduce this book or portions thereof in any form.

First printing: April 1987

A TOR Book

Published by Tom Doherty Associates, Inc.
49 West 24 Street
New York, N.Y. 10010

Cover art by Angus McKie

ISBN: 0-812-54433-1
CAN. ED.: 0-812-54434-X

Printed in the United States of America

0 9 8 7 6 5 4 3 2

This book is for
Fritz Reuter Leiber

ACKNOWLEDGMENTS

The author thanks the following for writing space, inspiration, and/or criticism: J. Berls, Professor N. Chomsky, Professor B. Foorman, Professor R. Fouts, R. Harre, University of Houston, University of Hokkaido, University of Kyoto Primate Installation, Linacre College, M. Lloyd, S. Martens, Professor H. Putnam, Hotel Satimatai, Professor Sugiyama, D. Yates, and, of course, Moja, chimpanzee.

PODZIĘKOWANIA

The Strange Creature ────

By and by we are called to Sir W. Battens
to see the strange creature that Captain
Holmes hath brought with him from Guiny;
it is a great baboone, but so much like a man
in most things, that (although they say there
is a Species of them) yet I cannot believe
but that it is a monster got of a man and a
she-baboone. I do believe it already understands much English; and I am of the mind
that it might be tought to speak or make
signs.

—Diary of Samuel Pepys
24 August 1661

THE TWO slowly crisscrossed the silent battle-
ground under the hot glare of the noon sun. A
thin strip of blue cloth showed from a laser
spotter's emplacement, flattened by an impact gre-
nade. The fat man nudged the blue cloth with his
stick. Bluebottles buzzed.

"No point opening that, brother man. That's uniform cloth."

Their own ranks were raggle-taggle—volunteers, humans, who had voted with their feet on the long march south. They wore the clothes they'd joined in. And the Battle of North Houston was their last. Now disappeared in air, in death and Mexican desert, the bizarre combination of super- and pseudo-science, publicity and plastic, mechanical intelligence and monkey mutation that had held a shrinking southwest against humanity, against natural man. The two men collected tags for the Memphis crèche. Identification tags, man tags. The oldest, made by the New York City crusaders at the beginning, were bare names scrawled by hand-held drill. The newest were stamped with the Seal of the Colorado Declaration Against the Non-Human, September 1, 2002.

Though the fat man walked on, the other levered up the hardened plastic roof that held the body of the blue cloth and the object of the bluebottles' interest. A real man might be wearing a strip of something like Brazorian uniform. And maybe even a turncoat human was owed a final look.

Thing underneath wasn't a crusader and it wasn't one of their crazy, armed robots. A robot that could in theory kill hundreds of humans apiece. A robot that an agile ten-year-old human could short out by hand, dodging in to snuff the wildly firing robot like a mongoose dispatching a cobra. Anyone who'd played a few games of Dodg'em Robot at a fun park could manage it.

Thing underneath was ripped apart form neck to crotch, uniform fled to the spread extremities, the mess of wrist and ankle. The whole body cavity opened; pale lungs framed purpling heart and blackening liver, skirted by swelling, translucent intestine. The upper half of a collar circled the throat but there was no chain or tag.

The man looked at the day-old corpse.

Then amid a swatch of blue he saw the long heavy straight black hair that nearly covered the pale white flesh of a forearm. A too long forearm. Though the crushed fingers were human enough, the forearm was wrong. The man spasmed and levered the roof clean aside. The head, chimpanzee, flopped forward. He heard a click, like the click of a photographic escapement, as he let the plastic down. He made the sign of the cross unthinkingly. But surely he meant no more superstition than allegiance to humanity demanded. A humankind H and a Christian T are not that different. The click could have been a robot or it could have been his imagination.

He remembered when he was a kid of seven and he realized that some mechanism was taking a picture of him half the minutes in the day. Robots and computers making a misery out of human life. Starting with the city kids on the streets, crazy-hooked on combat computer games, half playing killer robot, half playing gene-hyped chimpanzee, both giving mythic proportions to the clumsy but fashionable domestic robots, and labor chimpanzees, which had taken away so many human jobs. 'Course, hardly their fault, like the merciful human says. Ain't a machine say that the machines take the factory jobs. Ain't the apes say that the apes will pick the berries from the field and the coal from the deep faces. All

11

really just humans being bad to humans by not being human.

But no more.

All North America was clear of non-human, of false-made mechanical life and gene spawn. The rest of the nations with us, though maybe not as strict. The Nimburg Laws were firm. If only he did not somehow hear that escapement. The Nimburg Laws were earthwide. Nature reestablished. Without those mechanical telltale clicks. His eyes panned over the torn land to the horizon. What if there were a camera that pictured all that had happened?

Would the camera have a human eye?

1 Later Historical Developments ————

Tarzan, Lord Greystoke, was a fiction of the early twentieth century. An Englishman, raised by apes in the jungle, he seems perhaps an imaginative anticipation of later historical developments. "Nature imitates Art" as Oscar Wilde wrote.

—An Anthropologist's Notes, Frame I

THEY ATTACKED a woman and her Vegan Siamese cat last week. Gene-altered Vegan Siamese were "unnatural." They "offended the genetic order" and "the primacy of natural man." The woman was the Vegan ambassador to the Ecological Syndics. Big stuff.

The customs attendants had piled in hard to save the two of them. The ambassador and her cat survived quite unscathed, but one attendant and three Man Firsters were hospitalized, while a half dozen of the more obstreperous MFers were marched off in temporary arrest, chanting the Humanist Credo of prohibitions. No anthropoid Apes, No genetic Bastards, No thinking Computers, No human Degradation, . . . all the way through to No mind Transplants, and beyond that to No humans Unnatural, No synthetic Vitality, No artificial Wombs, No Lunisolar Year, No Xenophilia, and No Zoanthropy. All chanted in staccato hoots that reminded one of an animal pack raucously communing. Candy's Rigilians—now that's something that would really set them barking.

As the Houston Space Port flicker slid to a stop, I saw two attendants close on an MFer who stood, proud and ready, next to the medplan UPDATE-YOUR-TAPES poster. The MFer had spray-covered the poster in big, black letters with the MAN FIRST AND LAST motto. I sometimes forgot that the MFers even objected to mind implants as unnatural. Unconsciously my hand had been feeling along my baggy slacks. Nothing showed. In reality nothing could have shown the MFers that I was an implant.

Of course I was being silly. There was only the one MFer. Caped in a wrinkled black overcloak, he crowed out "Natural man first and last/Natural man first and last," while the attendants wrote out a ticket: He was hardly a danger.

After they handed him the ticket, he gave the attendants the humanist salute. Palm topped with the rigidly erect index and middle finger pointed straight up, crossed by the index finger of the left hand to form an H. It was hard to keep the index and middle fingers both parallel and apart. You got the logician's sign for *all*, rather than an H. So, as Candy once suggested, you could see it as two signs, *Humanity (is) All*, or *Universal Humanity*, or even *Humanity Über Alles (Humanity Over Everything*, the motto of New Praetoria). But this MFer hardly looked like a logician.

I followed the attendants to the flicker platform exit while the MFer tore his ticket to shreds.

I looked back once more at him. He had slung his black cloak more comfortably. There was an air of quaintness and resignation about him. I was tempted to tell him that I remembered once having a muscular, stately male body. Though my name is Sally, Sally Forth, now, and I have a well-functioning female body, albeit one with one odd feature.

I was tempted to tell him that I was an implant this past year or so and would otherwise be dead. All two of us. I was tempted to tell him that and ask him why he wanted me dead.

Bad temptations! Foolish temptations! Can't reason with an MFer. Officially, MFers just strongly oppose mind taping and implantations. If you happen to be the product of this evil procedure, you're a freak, an unnatural golem, an inhuman ape, but a monster to be pitied and prayed for. A monster in theory better dead, better never made, but a monster not to be violenced by the oh-so-righteous Man Firsters.

Officially, that's what the MFers say, but they also say that you really can't expect a red-blooded human being to put up with an implant. And a lot of times a lot of individual MFers have not put up with things in a rather nasty way.

15

I let the attendants get ahead of me and onto the slideway tunnel to the escalators that lift you to the floor of the Houston Camera, a vast dome that stretches some twelve stories up to the surface, ringed by stylish shops, eating places, and offices. I had to meet Candy at the northern edge of the rotunda's floor level, where interplanetary travelers exited customs and migration. But Candy wouldn't glide-in for twenty-five minutes. Customs and migration would double that time easily.

With the attendants out of sight I took the personnel lifter up to the sub-surface and climbed the last twenty meters up one of the landing crew stairs. Unless a place is really security conscious, a confident manner will get you there unquestioned. Of course you do have to know how to get there. But there now was just the open air and I had enough of a sense of places like this to know how to get up top to the landing surface. My body had some reflexes, some stored routines, for problems like this.

Not my mind, you understand. Or not my mind anyhow firsthand. My body has the reflexes of the life of an asteroid miner, and her reflexes sometimes seep into my conscious mind. When I want to do something that my spacer body knew how to do I just lean back and let the old body do its stuff—and my mind somehow comes up with words for what my body does. Eerie. Like being in occasional contact with a previous existence or a collective unconsciousness.

Interrupted only by the cluster of instruments that

decked the landingbay-control area, the sun-baked, flat, lush, almost marshy land of Brazoria stretched as far as I could see. Some twenty miles southeast I found the faint, smoggy halo of ancient Houston with its priceless historical district, the only extensive group of pre-twenty-first century buildings north of Old Mexico.

I almost fancied I could see the Plaza Hotel, center of ancient Houston's most exotic district, the Montrose. I knew where to look for the Plaza Hotel because it was near the much larger and much newer Norbert Weiner Research Hospital. And I could see NWRH. That was where I worked and lived. The Montrose is where you play.

Here, right along the edge of the glide-in pathways, were the verdant, feverish, northern limits of the Brazoria Republic of Texas, one hundred years in the dust of history. Here the North American Madness hordes had been held back by the crazy Brazoria Texans, assisted by an odd amalgam of computers, AI robots, a few score alpha-chimpanzees, and the several thousand so-called "machine sympathizers" and "anti-humanists" who escaped from the north.

I could see a pyramid-shaped monument nearby, another half a kilometer to the west, and another perhaps, beyond it farther west. The same to the east.

The monument had a disheveled look. The slideway didn't pass within reading distance. Even in cooler weather there would be few people up here. I imagined this monument was just a duplicate of its fellows, apparently stretching from east to west at

17

half kilometer intervals. As I walked closer I could see that the plaque had that pseudo-roman type that was used on everything from shop signs to gravestones in the middle of the twenty-first century, and on nothing since. The plaque was lettered in big capitals except for the note at the end.

HERE, ON JANVARY FOVRTH, 2001, OUR FELLOW HVMANS CLASHED TRAGICALLY, IN FVLL HVMANHOOD. THIS POINT MARKS THE SOVTHWARDMOST HIGH TIDE OF THE NORTH AMERICAN VISIONARIES. "THEIR ETERNALLY HVMAN VISION—SO TRAGICALLY IMPRACTICAL, SO FINALLY VICTORIOVS"—WILLIAM JENNINGS BRYANT TARNOVSKI. THIS POINT ALSO MARKS THE FINAL DEFENSE LINE OF THE VALIANT BVT MISGVIDED HVMANS OF THE BRAZORIAN REPVBLIC OF TEXAS (1997–2001). HERE STOOD THE ARMY OF BRAZORIA, MAJORGENERAL AND PRESIDENT OF THE REPVBLIC, LORD GETTY-GREYSTOKE, COMMANDING. (It is a matter of historical cvriosity that the last "alpha-chimpanzee" was destroyed on this perimeter. Since these noxiovs, gene-altered "alpha-chimpanzees" were the last known members, natvral or laboratory-spawn, of the biologi-

cal family, here was destroyed the last anthropoid ape.)

So "all the humans were valiant." In the secure
humanist times of the plaque's composition they had
called it the North American Vision, not the North
American Madness. The plaque composers had to
approve of both sides.

The lower-case note at the end of the plaque was
not in raised type. I smudged over both "was destroyed" and replaced them with "died." I would
tell Go-go about this.

Today was March 31, 2113, nearly a hundred
years since the general ratification of the Concordat
of Tokyo came to replace nation states with the
benign, or at least boring, rule of the Ecological
Syndics and the subordinate checker-boarding of the
Federation Commissions.

A couple of personnel looked west. I picked out a
fast-approaching speck, the winged packet boat on its
glide-in path. The last I had heard from Candy was a
pre-print abstract that hinted that the previous research on Rigilian intelligence was blown. Botched
experimental design. Something was wrong with our
basic thinking about the Rigilians. Maybe they had
no real intelligence.

I found I cared about this. Cared enough to pick
Candy up here to hear about it. Would have been out
here even if we weren't friends.

I had had hopes for the Rigilians. Hopes that these
reclusive, delicate octopoid creatures could talk with
us about ourselves.

I remembered that I hadn't really thought about the Rigilians when Candy had first mentioned them to me. That was close to a year ago on our supposed trip to the planet Rim. Dream therapy time. During the psychological half of the implantation procedure that had made me a living, thinking being, a wed of Sally Cadmus's body and Ismael Forth's mind.

I was curious now about non-human intelligence. And it wasn't simply ruminating on my own peculiarities.

No, Go-go and Golem made the difference.

The packet boat settled, quietly, gracefully, into the foreground, the three chutes that had blossomed behind her now sagged. She had slowed from a 400-kilometer landing speed to a standstill in less than 600 meters. Jet planes reverse their engines. But for a packet boat, glide-in chutes provide a lighter and more stable solution than brakes or a fore jet. She radiated surface heat.

Her glide-in flight from Space Station Zebra had produced less atmospheric pollution than the burning of a small bush. The same distance and angle from the center of Houston as this space port, but to the southeast of the city, you can visit the NASA museum and see the first space ship. It measures, literally, ten times the length of a modern packet boat, ten thousand times the weight, and produced a million times the atmospheric pollution, counting up flights as well as downs. Dirty air those days. But they still had orangutans back then, and gorillas and blue whales, and cheetahs, too, as fast as the wind.

The packet boat sank into one of the landing bays. In a few minutes I would have to think about getting down to the customs and migration exit. With the lowering of the packet boat the last of the personnel disappeared. Nothing but the glide-in paths, endless scrub and marshy land, and me. Humans below and everywhere in this swollen planet.

I saw her, coming through the press. I stood at the final customs barrier.

The old MFer with the wrinkled black overcloak stood near this side of the barrier. I had not seen the MAN FIRST stenciled on the back of his coat. One of the attendants eyed him warily. After the melee with the ambassador last week, some MFers had sworn vengeance.

The attendant's eyes left the MFer and patrolled the arriving passengers. Nervous.

Even at a distance I could see Candy Darling had filled out in the past year. Long, straight blond hair sweeping back over the shoulders of her bright, yellow tolong, the piercingly blue eyes. I remembered her flat rib cage and startlingly well-defined ruby nipples. The stringy eleven-year-old body had blossomed into a twelve-year-old combination of grace and gawkiness, all aglow with puberty. My friend was beautiful.

She also had someone in tow, or towing. A shyly belligerent-looking guy in his forties, the sort of guy who is either a mathematician or mentally subnormal, and, either way, something of a child, no matter how old. He clenched Candy's flight bag in his left hand. He seemed to regard it as a prize and his own suitcase as a battering ram. He doggedly pushed through the crowd toward the customs barrier, whirling his head around at intervals to assure himself that Candy followed in his wake.

He nearly decapitated an august matriarch with suitcase when I caught Candy's eye. She winked and gave a shrug of amused helplessness. Her bulldozer, having cleared the matriarch from their path, had now turned and, catching Candy's look, glared short-sightedly in my direction. He waved at me with one hand and then pointed toward the customs barrier with the other. I didn't realize until a little later that his gesture would have looked like an H to the barrier attendant. A glaring H. An unfriendly, Man Firster, H.

Then Candy's bulldozer drove forward through the final stretch for the barrier. The apprehensive attendant—Oriental with clipped, graceful gestures—held out his hand for the customs baggage ticket. But Candy's bulldozer would have none of that. I could see the attendant's startled face when the bulldozer moved forward, his battered suitcase first.

The trouble was that the flight bag had MF in large letters across it. ("Damn it," the bulldozer was to say later, "the scouts put that on. It abbreviates Martens' Fellow of Logic, the only Martens' Professorship New College has.") Unfortunately, the barrier attendant wasn't English, or Oxonian, and one of his fellows was still in the hospital after last week's clash.

22

"We've had quite enough of that, man," said the bulldozer. He brandished the bag. The attendant stiffened as he realized that the H-signing, MF-brandishing bulldozer had no ticket and was prepared to ram the case in his face. Candy waved the ticket from behind the bulldozer. But the Oriental attendant could not see her. Knees slightly bent, he prepared his hands to throw the supposed MFer into the middle of next week. This looked like it was going to work out badly.

II That Has Such People ——

When Shakespeare's Miranda, who grew up alone with her father on a magical island, first sees other human beings, she says, with evident delight, "Oh, brave new world, that has such people in't." In the twentieth century, the phrase "brave new world" became a label for morbid fears about the future.

—An Anthropologists's Notes, F. II

SOMEHOW I caught the attendant's eye and put my whole face and body into a dismissive posture that suggested that it wasn't important, that he forget it. That the bulldozer wasn't an MF rioter. The attendant relaxed, nodded at me, and turned aside. My right hand was at my crotch. I wondered whether I was giving something away. The bulldozer strode through the barrier, Candy in his wake. The bulldozer turned and glowed at Candy. A startlingly cherubic smile broke over his heavy face.

"You gotta be tough with them sometimes, Candice," he said. "Most of these jokers are just trying to make trouble for you."

Candy was in my arms, her newly prominent breasts against mine. "He's a bit strange but he can be a real sweetie—and he's incredibly bright," Candy whispered in my ear. And then she introduced us.

"Sally, this is Stanislaus Mummett. He sat next to me on the packet coming down. He does number stuff.

"And Stan, this is Sally Forth. She's my mother, sort of."

Stanislaus Mummett *did numbers* indeed. The meta-mathematical laboratory at MIT had three names engraved on its four pediments: Kurt Godel, A. Tarski, Mashima Hirosawa. There was a curiously persistent joke to the effect that the blank fourth pediment was reserved for Stanislaus Mummett.

His stubby fingers shook as he extended his hand. His heavily lidded and thickly glassed eyes goggled at me, and the cherubic grin reappeared. His hands always shook, I came to find, and he refused to allow any sort of medical corrective. The meta-mathematical institute might not need to wait long. He looked me up and down. Mostly down. There was some line of haunch. But I kept my pants baggy for concealment.

"I am happy to meet the mother of Candice. Even the 'sort of' mother."

"Well," said Candy. "I am sort of Sally's mother too."

Candy had been playing her standard little-girl role with him. But she was on the edge of coming out. They would make an interesting couple. Two bizarre combinations of youth and age. Behind Stanislaus Mummett's heavy face and childish grin I felt on me two penetrating eyes. My tail felt strange.

"Why don't you two pick up the rest of your baggage?" I said. "And then we can have a drink or something before taking the flicker. That is if . . ."

"Yes," said Mummett, "That's a grand idea."

The two of them toddled off. I looked back at the attendant. He had been glancing over to us from time to time. Or, rather, glancing at me. I had some apologies to make.

"Sorry about the big guy," I said to the attendant. "He gets worked up and silly. Thanks for laying off."

The attendant grinned. "I didn't recognize you were signing for a millisec. You without a suit on. I was just a steward on F.S. *Daedalus* a couple of years back. But I can recognize the *emergency* and *wait* signs. I've never seen anybody snap them off faster. I thought you were an agent. Trouble we been having with the MFers lately. You understand I thought he was some crazy Man Firster. At first."

The attendant made a circle with his thumb and index finger, the other fingers straight up and spread. I recognized it as a spacesuit work sign meaning *okay*—or *yes, I agree, let's do it*, etc., depending on situation. And then I realized that I had signed to the attendant.

I thought I had been putting a lot of expression in my face when I tried to head off the confrontation between Mummett and the attendant. But I had also put my right hand just behind my head, then brought

26

it down diagonally across my torso, and ended with my hand covering my crotch. That was why I had ended up wondering why my hand was there, though I dropped the matter when Candy introduced me to Stanislaus Mummett. (When I brought my hand down across my body that meant *freeze* or *stop* or even *no*, same as a diagonal line across a diagrammatic image of a smoking cigarette means no use of cannabis. The attendant apparently missed that sign. But he had caught the last one. A handchop to the crotch of your space suit meant wait. So that was why my hand ended up down there.)

But I have to get back to Candy Darling and her new friend Stanislaus Mummett. I fear for his virginity. Not for Candy's certainly. Candy is going on ninety mentally. Much nearer senility than innocence.

III Suppose the Native ———

I suppose the native, any native—us—ought to look at the issue of alien intelligence by asking: *Are the alien intelligences likely to find our existence improbable?*

—An Anthropologist's Notes, F. III

"SO THIS dumb-bunny said to me that there couldn't be any Extra-Terrestrial Intelligences. Candice, can you imagine anything more foolish?" Stanislaus Mummett's eyes took on a glazed look.

Apparently spurred by an interest in Candy, Mummett decided to stop in Houston. Indeed he'd already registered at Candy's hotel, the LBJ Houston. So he and Candy sent their baggage on from the space port to the hotel and we settled down over champagnedaccas in a cozy, dimly lit booth in the Kyoto Gardens Saloon.

Hologrammatic projections isolated our small table and the circle we formed around it with a mysteriously shimmering wall of color, our faces clearly though gently illuminated, the rest a soft romantic dimness. Mummett had on clothes only accidentally related to the lumpy contours of his body, or to any consideration of style, practicality, comfort, or sanitation. Any form of apparel had but to be put on him for a few minutes to become disheveled and unappealing. He merely triumphantly anticipated this development by his choice of clothing.

Mummett continued. "Couldn't be E.T.I.'s, because if they were genuinely intelligent they would have advanced technology. And with advanced technology their planets would put out so much patterned electro-magnetic activity that we would pick them up. Or they would have picked us up and come hopping here. Or, supposing they lacked a way into our local wormhole circuit—'the lonely five-point pyramid that is all we can travel'—why surely they would send an unmistakable message."

Mummett paused to drain his champagne-dacca. He stared at the empty glass, pressed the waiter call button, and then threw the glass backward over his head. A plastic hand with another champagne-dacca emerged from the shimmer that surrounded us. Mummett had the glass before the hand lowered it to the table.

"Perfect, damn, absolute fool. Of course, it's true that you can pick out a simple, low-power shortwave broadcast—just the ordinary folk flooding the local airways—across half the galaxy. You could . . . so let's calculate. . . ."

Mummett removed his thick glasses and goggled briefly into that logician's distance, that fairy dance of mind far vaster and richer than all the contents of our physical universe. I tuned out until he wrote on the table.

> CHANCE OF PICKING UP INTELLIGI-
> BLE E.T.I. BROADCAST IN PAST TWO
> HUNDRED YEARS (OPTIMUM CONDI-
> TIONS): .2

"So there might be a reasonable chance one way or the other of picking them up if we had had optimum conditions. *But we didn't and we don't.*"

Mummett's handwriting was cramped but strangely graceful and precise. His hands did not shake at this.

"Sagan and some other guys did something like a few weeks of it back in the twentieth century. And after the Nimburg Laws collapsed a few decades back we've run a couple of long surveys—over humanist objections. And we found that someone did a few hours of survey on the sly back when computers were under ban. All of which means changing a reasonable possibility to a million to one shot." Here Mummett once again assaulted the table paper. Like many mathematicians educated in the Nimburg period he took pride in operating without a computer.

> CHANCE OF PICKING UP INTELLIGI-
> BLE E.T.I. BROADCAST IN TWO HUN-
> DRED YEARS (ACTUAL CONDITIONS):
> .00006

"So I told this joker that there's practically no chance we'd have picked up evidence of intelligent life if it's out there. Even if there is lots of it out there. Could be several hundred planets and we still wouldn't have picked 'em up. Of course, if there're a thousand planets with intelligent life, all looking around, chances are they'd pick each other up. And maybe us too for that matter. Chances are, you'd hope, that they all won't be chauvinistic like us humans. I got some ideas about that.''

Then something odd happened. Suddenly Mummett's face emptied of expression, motionless as a stone Buddha. His voice, literal and frighteningly certain, was not for us. "They're out there," he said. "They're out there. Taking pictures and making tapes or whatever they do. I know they're out there. Yet how to tell them. . . .'' Mummett returned to us.

"So I had to concede to this joker—not that the humanist dumb-bunny would have thought of it—that if there's a lot of intelligent life out there, they just might have noticed us humans. But then I pointed out to him, there just wouldn't be any plausible reason for them to want to get in touch with us. With *us?* Boring. Distasteful.

"Besides—'' Mummett's eyes narrowed and his face curled into a deranged look that I eventually realized was intended as artful cunning. He winked at Candy. "Besides, I told 'im, 'How do you know they haven't picked us up long ago and placed Earth and the other inhabited Federation planets—all paltry five of them—behind a screen?' ''

Mummett surged upward half out of his seat for emphasis, knocking a bowl of imitation Rigil nuts into the hologram of Houston Space Port that reared up from the middle of our table.

"How do you know I'm not an E.T.I.?" Mummett raised his eyebrows over his thick glasses and heavy eyelids. He goggled his eyes dramatically.

" 'How do you know?' I told 'im. 'How do you know I'm not an E.T.I.? Sent to make sure you jokers don't find out there's a universe of sensible creatures out there who don't want to be bothered by human chauvinist swine?' "

I winked at Candy, rolling my eyeballs in Mummett's direction. Mummett's beefy, sallow, and misshapen face, particularly with his goggling expression, did suggest something outside human space. That would be one way he could know—no talk of probabilities there—they were out there. By being one of them. Except that, come to think of it, that would make them in here, too. There was something in the way that Mummett had said *I know* that sent a tingle up the spine.

Fortunately, Mummett chose this moment to give his attention to fishing some Rigil nuts out of the hologrammic miniature of the Port's grand rotunda. Candy visibly forced a laugh into a closed-lip grimace and kicked me under the table. Reflexively, my tail was out of my pants and I'd made a grab for Candy's ankle that just missed.

When I wear slacks, my tail goes down my left leg, the finger-thumb on the end into the top of my boot. But Rostards makes slacks with a quick release seam that opens from my boot to my crotch with a practiced flick of my meter-long prehensile tail.

32

Obviously puzzled, Mummett stalled, his hand holding Rigil nuts over the hologram in the center of the table. His right hand was circuited every few seconds by a packet boat, improperly both gliding-in and ascending and looking for all the world like a gnat. Mummett, given his thick glasses and slightly walled eyes, managed the feat of staring at both of us at once. Then he coughed, collected himself, and looked into his right hand, giving an air of wondering at its contents.

"Rigil nuts," I said.

"No," he said, a grin percolating across his face. "No, you're nuts. These are imitations, grown here. No, you are the nuts." He generously included Candy in the category by a cast of his hand.

"You are the Rigil nuts," continued Stanislaus Mummett, giggling. Had he and Candy talked about the Rigilians? No, she was still playing the twelve-year-old innocent.

"Anyhow, I told this joker that I was actually a five-legged pentagon from Westen Punkt, Sirius Sector, just maintaining my visual appearance by clouding his mind telepathically." Mummett chased his handful of imitation Rigil nuts with a long pull of champagne-dacca.

"Indeed, I offered to prove to him I was E.T.I. Of course, I explained that my actual appearance was just too frightening for 'im—my purple, slime-flecked fangs especially, you understand—so I wasn't going to drop my telepathic shield, purely out of consideration for 'im. But I was going to show 'im another way." Mummett rummaged in his pocket and came up with a cherry-sized ball bearing. He handed it to Candy, who took it in her agile and surprisingly powerful hands. Hands which had once been for me the only odd part in the appearance of a slim eleven-year-old, blue-eyed blonde.

"Now, Candice, I'll show you what I showed him, how I could read his mind. Put your hands below the table, where you were fooling around just a second ago, and show me your fists without telling me which one has the ball bearing." So instructed the Mummett, obviously enjoying himself, though his hands as always shook like relaxo-vibrators. Candy fronted her fists.

Mummett closed his eyes and knotted his brow as if in deep concentration. "Ah, yes, yes . . . I see. . . . Keep your hands still, Candice, keep them still. . . . Stop fighting my mind. . . . Okay, yes . . ." and so on. Finally he opened his eyes and reached forward toward her fists, weaving his eyes slightly to one side and then the other as he neared.

"This is the one, the one you think of as right." Mummett leaned forward and tapped Candy's right hand and indeed she opened it to show the ball bearing. I gave Candy an *oh-wow* look adrip with skepticism over Mummett's shoulder. Candy nudged me under the table and gave Mummett her best twelve-year-old girlish smile.

"Uncle Stan, you must have peeked or something."

"Uncle Stan" Mummett pretended to bristle at that. He insisted on making a blindfold from his napkin. After some ineffective fumbling on his part I managed to get it securely around his eyes.

His hands felt surprisingly warm. And shaking. Whatever kind of trick he might be playing on Candy and me could not depend on dexterity.

After he had "read" Candy's mind, I was expected to lift his blindfold so that he could see to pick the hand that Candy's mind told him contained the ball bearings.

As Mummett went through his "Ah, yes . . . I see. . . ." mumbo jumbo, I reflected on how transparent it really was. Of course you could tell your subject to keep his hands still. Anybody with hands out like Candy's would move them a bit or think that they had. And that stuff about not fighting his mind was a classical trap for the gullible—tell them to stop what they don't know how to tell they're doing and to stop fighting something that they don't know how to recognize.

When ordered, I pushed up Mummett's blindfold and watched his right hand waver from one to the other and again fix on the hand in which Candy held the ball bearing. Magic tricks work through misdirecting your attention, I reasoned.

Nothing could be going on during the mumbo jumbo period. Could it be that Mummett watched Candy's hands as his hand wavered between them and picked the one that gave it away, the one that perhaps could be made to flinch a bit? Most magic tricks depend on diverting your attention by mumbo jumbo, and some depend on the subject (the dupe) giving away the game with an unconscious gesture. Frankly I wondered whether Stanislaus Mummett had the sleight of hand for the maneuver I imagined.

Candy evidently bought my hypothesis, for she demanded that Mummett "Do it again!" with the blindfold on all the time. I didn't know how Mummett worked it. I did know that he was enjoying himself enormously. He had a grin on like a cat who has made free of the chicken hutch. The feathers dangled.

Again the mumbo jumbo, in which Stan Mummett had some difficulty maintaining solemnity. He looked so unlike a master of the ancient mystical arts. A big, clumsy, disheveled man, heavy, flabby jaw out one end of the blindfold and from the other, greasy hair sticking out in all directions. Was there a *disheveled Buddha* in the Asian pantheon?

A laugh began to break upward from my belly when Candy kicked away at me once more. This time I was ready. My tail grabbed her ankle as she pulled it back. I had the finger-thumb end of it locked in the shank, the whole noosed around Candy's wriggling ankle. Candy cut off the beginnings of a yip. Mummett, whose right hand had now moved out over Candy's fists, paused. But Candy, sticking her tongue out at me and trying to yank her foot from my grasp, kept her fists in place over the table in front of her.

You have to understand that although Candy is nearly ninety-five she loves hamming it up in a twelve-year-old body. Else why would she be one of the two dozen or so nymphers in the Federation? Someone has got to be crazy for the feel of childhood and puberty to run the shock and risk of implantation.

Candy and I loved to play around. And we hadn't seen each other for close to a year. And we loved each other. And Candy was the harmonizer, the one who brought me through the psychic end of my implant operation, who played the other, friend and mother, to the coalescing bits and pieces of personality and neurology that came to make me.

Mummett's right hand wavered over Candy's fists. Still attempting to free her foot, Candy yanked so hard that my tail's tip was close under her fists and Mummett's hand, separated by a few inches of air and a half inch of table. Suddenly I felt it. Something like a tickle of low amperage current and a taste of sour horseradish.

All from the tail tip of course, by far the most sensitive part of my tail, and strangely sensitive. I still haven't got all of it down though I've had the tail for over a year.

Those with tails can complain about my description. Otherwise just take it that that's how it felt. For a long time after my operation fried potatoes and onions on my tongue made me feel as if my nipples were being sucked. Erotic hash. A hard business to tune body and mind together, the tail just a part of it. Eerie.

But I knew what was causing the electric horseradish sensation in my tail's tip. Uncle Stan was supplementing the old mystical mumbo jumbo with some modern scientific gadgetry. I had learned that my tail electric-radished at the touch of various kinds of electro-magnetism. Uncle Stan Mummett used a device which projected an electro-magnetic field to tell which hand held the ball bearing. Almost certainly something just within the right hand sleeve of his jacket. Hah!

When I let go of her ankle, Candy had just opened her hand to show so that Mummett, already half standing, leaned much farther forward, reaching out his right hand as if to assist her. I whipped my tail around the side of the table and grabbed. Mummett hurtled himself backward with a shout as if bitten by a snake. I enjoyed that. Pleasures of the tail.

And I held in triumph over the table, between the finger-thumb of my tail's end, the black, lighter-sized device that Mummett had had clipped inside his right sleeve. The radish tingle was strong but not unpleasant. I waved my tail leftward and then back and forth through the Houston Space Port hologram, which rainbow sparkled and blacked out and then repaired its illusion as I moved Mummett's telltale through it.

Candy applauded.

"Thus biology triumphs over metallic electronics," I said.

"Hydro-carbon chauvinist," retorted Mummett, having just caught his breath.

And then he began to cry.

IV Tell Tails

What became the bird's flying apparatus first developed as a cooling device. The dolphins' "fins" were once forelegs. Evolution endlessly adapts old parts to new conditions, like a tar-paper-and-bailing-wire handyman. The same is true of words. So the punster is a linguistic evolutionist, showing us not the mammalian hand in the bat's wing, but rather demonstrating the tale in the tail.

—An Anthropologist's Notes, F. IV

SUCCULENT CHICKEN teriyaki and a colorful spread of sushi with Vegan pickles, plus a fresh champagne-dacca, revived Stanislaus Mummett. Candy's idea. She pushed a chunk of chicken in his mouth and his jaws began to move, slowly and then into high gear. The stolid and forlorn look disappeared as did the sushi and teriyaki, all with increasing speed. An amazingly cherubic smile beamed outward between bites.

Even the guilt that I felt after my initial sense of triumph soon ebbed as I explained about my tail. The Mummett's tears, as with smaller-sized children, were impudently transitory. I told my story to a happy man.

"I had the tip of my tail up under the table near where you used your cheater. The tip just feels funny when there's a field nearby. The sort spy and sensor devices put out. Only spacers have prehensile tails and some of them don't ever get the reaction. And others find it, you might say, a pain in the arse to react to because they're surrounded with electro-magnetic gadgets, so they learn to deaden out the sensation.

"I kind of like being able to feel things like that. And my psychetician—Germaine Means—she's al-ways said that getting into my tail helps me with the implant. That and occupational therapy like working with Go-go."

I showed him the entirely hairless tip, ending in something like a powerful index finger and a rather small thumb. The rest of my tail is frosted with the same blondish fuzz as on my arms and nap (not the brown straight stuff on my head or the curly thick stuff at my torso joints). The muscles, giving it the thickness of a neonate's wrist, cover up the bones of a very flexible continuation of my spinal column—an artificially induced but otherwise natural prolongation of my coccyx.

Stan took the end of my tail in his pudgy hands without hesitation.

"What's it like to have a limb that other humans don't have, Sally?" said Stanislaus softly, stroking my tail. "And a kind of sensory apparatus we don't have, for that matter?"

I had to think about the answer to that.

On a life-bearing planet like Earth, the only primates with prehensile tails are those that can hang from them. Spider monkeys for example. And they can't be much more than five kilos or so or the tail would have to be monstrous in proportion to the rest of the body. Here on Earth I can't hold up my weight with my tail—let alone swing about with it. Still has its uses.

Spacers cover up their tails on Earth—and the other planets of the golden pyramid of manageable wormhole interstellar flight. And it's not just the Man Firster lunatic fringe who'd probably try to cut your tail off. Or, for that matter, the majority spectrum of more or less humanist persuasion who frown on bioprosthetic limbs, genetic tailoring, and attempted communication with E.T.I.'s, and who don't believe in non-human intelligence, whether biologic or artificial, Rigilian octopoid or ape, computer or Mummett's hypothetical star travelers.

No, apart from MFers and humanists, most people just aren't used to tails and feel queasy about them. But I don't now feel ashamed of my tail as I sometimes did in the therapy period after my implant. Momma here is happy and proud of every bit of her.

I was a creature of coincidence. The Ismael Forth body had been obliterated in the once-in-a-billion

41

freak diving accident that modern safety technology didn't stop. So they took the fortunately updated Ismael Forth neurological structure tape—like the data disks of a main frame—and went looking for something extremely rare, a healthy body with a blanked brain.

Two years before, and half a solar system away, Sally Cadmus's tiny mining ship was blown up by a meteor collision that left her with enough space-suit fuel to jury-rig herself into a Hohmann orbit. An orbit that would have her intersect with Earth's ring of space stations in a little less than two years. But she had only enough oxygen to keep her body alive in the sort of low temperature hibernation that would randomly leak her mental structure into blankness like the random access memory of an inadequately charged computer. And Sally Cadmus hadn't updated her tapes.

So wild coincidence and human artifice—Germaine Means, Candy Darling, François Vase, and the whole crew—put me together, mind and body we. I could hardly claim to be natural. Any more natural than the first strand of DNA that teased out its marvelous structure from randomly writhing amino acid as if a volcano had spat into the cooling water a perfect Parthenon, pedestals to friezes. The tail was the least of it, as pleasing and as alienating as it may be. I am the only one who can tell this story. Mind and body, soft and hardware, we.

"You know," I replied, "right after initial implant all the connections between mind and body scramble.

Mustard on my tongue felt like you hit my funny bone. Everything had to be tuned together to avoid rejection. The tail is just part of it.

"In space, in weightlessness, I can do acrobatics with my tail. Lovely stuff, call it space larking. Here on Earth it's an extra hand."

I was brought back from my reverie by a comment of Stan's that straightened up Candy and me like a shot.

"Yes, Sally," said Mummett softly, "why don't you tell me about Go-go, and Kay-kay and Golem for that matter. And then Candy can tell us both about the Rigilians.

"Maybe after that I'll have a proposition to make to you two," said Professor Stanislaus Mummett. The chicken feathers once more dangled from his huge lopsided grin.

And then I realized that Mummett hadn't shown the slightest curiosity about my mention of an implant. He hadn't asked why or how I happened to have a tail, only what it felt like. And that crack about Candy and me being Rigil nuts. He knew everything about us. Maybe he really did know that the alien intelligences were out there. There had been no talk of probabilities when he issued that self-addressed judgment. Maybe somehow he knew.

Stanislaus Mummett was Putnam Professor of Mathematics at Harvard University and he had another like that at Oxford University over in England. I had to stop thinking of him as a fool however childish and bumbling the exterior—or interior.

If we had remained in the saloon for the accounts of Go-go and the Rigilians we might have never made it into Houston. So we bribed Mummett with the promise of an antique Brazoria barbecue in historic Montrose. I told the story of my friendship with Go-go in transit to the LBJ Houston Hotel.

V The First Anthropoid ─────

The first anthropoid that the United States sent into Earth orbit, Enos, performed perfectly on his computer panel even though malfunction often caused him to be electrically shocked as if he were making errors. After 1,263 hours of electroshock-governed training, Enos's blood pressure had increased from an average of 90 systolic to 200. Enos was permanently caged after postflight medicals. The second anthropoid, John Glenn, became a millionaire and senator after near deification in a New York City ticker-tape parade. The name "Enos" was provided for publicity purposes. The first anthropoid orbiter was known to his users only by a number.

—An Anthropologist's Notes, F. V

THE STORY of Go-go and me starts with that grand, crazy Lord Getty-Greystoke, Major-general and President of the Brazoria Republic, compatriot of computers and alpha-chimpanzees, whose body was found forty years ago, cryogenically stored with a chimpanzee companion in a reactor-run mausoleum cunningly hidden under the Brazoria River.

Or it starts with Allen and Beatrice Gardner, who first taught a chimpanzee, Washoe, sign language back in the twentieth century—their student Roger Fouts was killed defending the aged Washoe in the first breakout of the Man Firsters in 1989.

Or it starts with Germaine Means, who realized some ten years ago that, even if we still don't know how to unfreeze, repair, and restore those still intact human corpses that the twentieth century has bequeathed to us, we might just be able to unfreeze and clone up a single cell. But who would bother with a human cell in a planet so replete with humans? A planet purged of chimpanzees, orangs, and gorillas by a combination of human indifference and humanist chauvinism.

Or the story starts a half million years ago in some forest clearing where man beast gestured to man beast, perhaps holding out a stick shaped to poke out grubs from a tree branch or offering the pleasures of a berry-bearing bush? Or why not all the way back to that teasing original DNA strand minding its way from simple hydrocarbons to the stars? Assuming you're human, we share over 99.5 percent of our genetic structure with my chimpanzee friend Go-go. Or, to put it another way, 99.5 percent of what makes a human a homo sapiens, is exactly the same as the genetic stuff that makes a chimpanzee a chimpanzee. Vive la .5 percent! But bravo the 99.5 percent that makes us one. Kissing cousins.

Best begin when I met Go-go.

After the neurological restructuring, the second and much longer half of the implant operation is a form of psycho-physical drama in which body and mind are tuned together, tuned together through a story created by the harmonizers and the implant person's unconscious reactions. In my operation drama, the harmonizers—that's François Vase and Candy Darling—had me interact a lot with simulated animals. Perhaps that put the idea in Germaine Means's head.

And so after one week of convalescence—she was hardly one to let the grass grow under her feet or anyone else's—Germaine took me to Building 20, one of the outlying structures of Norbert Wiener Research Hospital. Building 20 was one of those ramshackle buildings with *Restricted Access—No Unauthorized Personnel* on all its doors. And an aura that says, *Important enough things go on here that we don't need to tart up our appearance or tell you what we do*.

Inside and down a hall, Germaine paused at a door and told me to come in and close the door when she said she was ready. *Take it slow and watch yourself.*

Minutes later I beheld the beast.

Germaine squatting, back to me, with a black hand, disproportionately long, over her right shoulder. To the left, peeped around that strangely wizened, strangely wise, strangely young, squash-nosed face, with magnetic, bright brown eyes.

Go-go moved more clearly into view, rounded his lips into an opening the size of a half-credit piece, and began a cheery hooting, first slow, tentative, and soft, gradually building in speed and loudness: hoot, Hoot, HOot, HOOt, HOOT, HOOT, *HOOT*, and so on. I felt answering hoots almost sucked from my lips, building, building, building to a joyous climax that set the walls of the laboratory ringing. I am a participator.

"You're the first visitor in months," Germaine explained. "Only six people from the Director NWRH on down know about the installation. Still want to be careful, even with the annulment of the Nimburg Laws. And you can't tell about the MFers anyway. I will publish eventually. In *Science* and *Kagaku-no Nikkan-shimbun*. I think then the shit will hit."

I got my knees on the floor as Go-go approached, supporting most of his weight on his back limbs, with a slight assist from forward. Those penetrating brown eyes inspected my face from a distance of less than a foot. Inspected it carefully, centimeter by centimeter, with an occasional, somewhat reassuring glance back into my grayish eyes.

Though Go-go weighed perhaps half my fifty-odd kilos, his hands were as wide as mine, and his fingers longer and, like his arms, considerably stronger. Oddly, his thumbs were smaller than mine, while the thumbs of his handlike feet were longer. From the moment I saw his hands close I was struck by their similarity to mine—the swirls of fingerprint patterns, the occasional hairs on the back of the inmost digit span, the smooth, under-pinked fingernails (we both already habitually bit ours, and nervously pushed the cuticles back). Nothing more pleased Go-go than the opportunity of so manicuring my fingernails, though I came to draw the line at biting.

Go-go carefully brought the nails of his index fingers together as he inspected my left cheek and nostril. His lips pursed and he pulled air in with a reflective, sustained kissing sound. Off went the top of the small pimple I had worried at in the mirror earlier that day. Germaine stood, a touch apprehensively, a touch proprietarily, a few meters away. I let Go-go proceed with his careful grooming.

My ears were carefully and intimately examined. I found it necessary to steer his fingernails away from a freckle on my forehead whose surgical removal didn't interest me. Those warm and reassuring eyes once more took mine in. There was little white. The iris, at close range, presented an intricate geometric pattern, ranging from dark brown to an iridescent light hazel, all dilating and contracting kaleidoscopically as Go-go glanced from my dark hair to my light skin and back again to my eyes.

My teeth were surveyed, the plaque buildup on my lower incisors experimentally nail-scraped. Finally my nose, my nostrils, were examined. The index fingernails once more in action, a hair was plucked.

I kept my nerve during these—what? A human might have said *these indignities*. These things one may not do. The more rebellious of us retreat to privacy to pick noses, pinch pimples, or bite nails.

Others avoid such entirely. I remember my mother—Ismael Forth's mother—occasionally picked at my blackheads in public when I was seven or eight. No greater indignity could have occurred to me then. I fully recognized even then that it would have been unspeakable for me to have picked my mother's pimples.

Yet with Go-go all was tit for tat. Grooming was no assertion of parental authority, nor indignity. As it might be for a less compulsive humanity, as it is occasionally and mildly among human lovers, grooming was a form of social interaction. Indeed, for Go-go, perhaps the norm of comradeship.

It was best for me, particularly when those powerful fingers gently probed the inside of my nose, that I did not know that Go-go, two-thirds my weight, could throw a heavy human fighter like a sack of Vegan candy beans. The forearms and hands, if anything slightly stronger than his legs, had strength that could make a steroid-hupped two-hundred-kilo sumo wrestler look like a flabby beach blowup toy—as I was to appreciate much later.

When he removed his fingers from my nose, Go-go pulled his upper lip up with one hand and, holding my eyes, pointed with the other hand to a small purplish spot on the gum just over a bicuspid. I worried the spot gently. Not knowing quite what to do I shifted attention to his hands. Feeling, gently pinching, pressing the cuticles back. With surprise I realized that though his hands, foreface, and handlike feet were black, the rest of his skin was white, whiter than mine. Though when you didn't look close, long straight thick black hairs covered up the white skin.

Go-go broke off my manicuring to lope, several-limbedly, across the lab to fetch a brush. Returning, he stroked once with his right fingers along his left forearm, and handed me the brush, pointing to his shoulder.

"He signed *brush me*," said Germaine. "Go ahead." Germaine smiled in what seemed a motherly fashion.

I brushed Go-go's shoulder. After a time he shifted position and pointed out new spots to be brushed. When I experimented in brushing a spot he did not point to, he turned his penetrating brown eyes to mine, and pulled the brush where he wanted. Soon I had covered much of his back, neck, head, and limbs.

Arms and hands disproportionately long and large, torso long too. Legs short and bowed as one who has field-labored his life in a squat position. In all this he was not unlike some human dwarfs. And yet of course Go-go was a perfectly natural chimpanzee, more prone to scooting along on the ground but as profoundly suited to swing from tree limb to tree limb, or from pillar to post, as I was to hurtling myself about in weightlessness. At least Go-go seemed a perfectly natural chimpanzee from all that Germaine had read and seen in twentieth-century books, journals, and films.

As I finished brushing Go-go, I realized that someone other than Germaine observed us. From behind a heavy wire partition peered Kay-kay, nearly two years old, long-legged and -limbed, more straight-backed and human-headed in appearance, half the weight of a thin human child of the same age though more agile.

One theorist Germaine read suggested that humans were like chimps whose genetic triggers did not fire them beyond the late childhood form. Though their form grew large in size, humans did not go on, as Go-go was beginning to, to the thickening of the skull ridges and heavy growth of shoulder and forearms of the adult ape. The human is just a permanently immature ape. (Our visions of the "next stage" in human evolution just extend this—we image a permanently infant-proportioned human, with the huge brain and diminutive limbs of babies.)

Are we not the same in root? Are we not the same except for lengthening for shortening, widening or thinning, of our parts? As if we apes were all as one except distorted in various ways—like forms seen in fun-house mirrors. I often think so. Even to the point of seeing poor dear Go-go as if in the flat mirror, while I am in the curved and dimpled one.

After all, we exterminated them, not they us.

After brushing my hair for a bit, Go-go began to take my clothes off. First my walking shoes. Unbuckled, carefully rebuckled a notch loose, unbuckled once more and removed. (I had pulled my tail tip back halfway up my calf, invisible.) Then the underankle pylon socks. The three buttons of my light tan dress jacket came next. Go-go put that aside and carefully looked over my loose slacks.

Go-go gave a glance over at Germaine and once again began his hoot-hoot series, first lip ovaling, eyes bright, then soft and slow, faster and louder, to a thundering climax. Again I joined in, feeling a release of the tension that had built up in me. With his last joyous hoot, Go-go quickly reached out to the back of my left calf, capturing my tail tip under the loose material of my slacks. Somehow Go-go had known something was there, perhaps because, having met but a half-dozen humans, Go-go had no reason to rule out a tail. You can imagine what Go-go wanted next. Germaine smiled, willing to play a tolerant parental role.

I stood up and let Go-go unclip and pull off my slacks. The lab was warm so I did not worry about shivering. At least from the cold. So there I stood before the ape in my blouse and sheer pylon under-briefs. I flicked my tail forward.

The careful concentration that Go-go had given my head and hands was eclipsed by the respectful attention given my tail, the hairless finger-thumb tip particularly. Go-go gently pushed back the tiny cuticle on the fingertip, eventually tonguing it lightly. When he tried to bite the diminutive nail I pulled back a bit. He went over the small thumb, setting me to work the articulation, then proving it himself reflexively. Once more, the hooting.

I was beginning to like Go-go. For all my anti-rejection therapy, for all the friendly wisdom of Germaine and Candy, no one had treated my tail with such unaffected intimacy and simple, friendly acceptance. Any beast in a brainstorm.

Go-go turned his back to me, readied himself, made a couple of abrupt hand signs that Germaine explained as *chase-tickle*, and we were off, scampering around the lab, from combination-locked refrigerator to the loft-bed ladder, from Klein-bottled beach bouncer to blackboard cubby. With increasing confidence I chased and tickled, causing a particularly riotous reaction when I tickled with my tail.

There was a symmetry of powers between us. I could pick up Go-go fairly easily. He was two-thirds my weight. And short enough to swing when I held him under the armpits—or even just above his elbows. But he was much stronger than I. Much stronger. And sometimes he could get too worked up.

Our chase-tickle game came to an end that first day when Go-go began to roll out a whole series—to be frank his best series—of signs. Food signs. *Banana*—run the tip of the index finger of your right hand along the length of the index finger of your left. *More*, as in *more banana*—arms out in front and parallel, bring your fists together again and again. *Drink*—fist with thumb slightly out, bring the thumbnail to your lips. And so on: *fruit, apple, sweet, juice, cereal, gator, coffee* (Germaine drank lots of it), *bread, carrot, orange*. The appetite for communication: you sign it and you get it.

Go-go shared his juice with me, carefully held the cup to my lips and tilted it to let a moderate flow into my mouth, then tilted back. The actions of my mouth so interested him that he would set the cup aside to gently raise my lip so he might see the inner actions. I remember sending Candy a coded cheap-statt account of my first days with Go-go. In her return flimsy from Rigil Gamma, some two months later, she wrote that I seemed to be Go-go's pet.

Go-go did not, however, share oranges or bananas. These he really prized. He enthusiastically fed me cereal. As Germaine heaved Go-go food, I suddenly realized that I felt hungry. It was 5:30 P.M. I had spent five hours with Go-go. The rush of intimate action made it seem like fifteen minutes—or fifteen days.

The next months swam with such action as I groomed and played with Go-go, built love and trust with Go-go, learned and eventually taught sign language and generally communed with him. Germaine was happy to have me. Of the small number of people who knew about Project Go-go, four had been sharing lab time, and one of those had been bitten seriously by Go-go and was afraid of him.

That first evening—Go-go within view, gently sighing in his sleep, covered by his splendid red blanket—Germaine and I sat in the glassed-in observation room, looking through the ancient records. The cracked, yellowed paper, the antique print, of the late twentieth-century books and journals. Stokoe's, and Bellugi and Klima's, guides to that now long dead American Sign Language (ASL).

In those days of inadequate medical technology, many humans were permanently deaf, so there were hand sign languages like ASL. Deep and complicated languages like our spoken ones today, or so Germaine learned from these ancient tomes. Not short, informal

55

expedients like the spacesuit slang of fifty or so gestures that my memory held.

The ape communication research had only been possible because languages like ASL were around. No one could have started it up today unless, like Germaine, they had stumbled on records of this ancient research. Go-go can hoot, and make that kissing-sucking sound, but that's it. No future for him in oral communication.

Germaine doesn't know whether Go-go is an ordinary chimpanzee or one of the genetically tailored alpha-chimpanzees that served in the Brazorian army. The alpha-chimpanzees were supposedly more talented at sign language than the ordinary chimpanzees of the first signing research. We did know that Go-go had done well. You could talk with Go-go.

VI Turing's Monster ——————

Alan Turing, who authored the basic theory of the computer and helped build the first ones, proposed that the first really capable computer should be equipped with a robot body, and then set free. He wondered what that computer would think of humans.

—An Anthropologist's Notes, F. VI

WHEN I returned to my room after that first golden day with Go-go I found Golem sympathetic but a little worried. After you got through the brattiness, that is.

Golem is, or is a creature of, the NWRH computer. He speaks in a cheeky, boyish voice and he's sneaky. Part of my implant therapy process. Plop down the cortical-neurological structure of a mind into a very different body. The thoughts of one and the reflexes of the other are not likely to be immediate friends. Golem had to be part of that complicated process, though I didn't know it while the therapy took place.

After my psychodrama tuning process, Candy left for Rigil. And Germaine introduced me to Golem. Golem the psychologist. Golem the brat. Golem the monstrously intelligent, creepy, brat kid brother.

"I hope you enjoyed sexing up that muscle-bound hunk of *schwarze* meat," said Golem from the ceiling general circuit receiver of my room. "And stripped to your little panties, too." Golem has video eyes and ears through the whole of NWRH. And elsewhere. Consider him God. Everywhere invisible, his immaterial voice ready to pop out anywhere. He normally talked to me in my room, though. People have interacted with CALTOKO line computers as if they were full-fledged thinking persons for decades. No one admits it though.

"Go-go isn't black," I replied hotly. "His skin is whiter than mine. François Vase is black. And Go-go isn't meat."

"François Vase isn't black," retorted Golem from the bedside speaker. "You couldn't even call him parboiled sienna. Black—black, by sol and little electricities—black is absolutely out of the question. Unadulterated carbon is black, black holes are black, your bedside lamp base is black, Go-go's hair is black, most of the buttons on my so-called control console are black. François Vase is light sienna shading into maple. He's about as black as you are white.

"And if Go-go isn't a hunk of meat, I don't know what is. Animal protein on the hand, balanced amino acid fuel, with fat and sugars for seasoning. Mince him up and charcoal broil, and you couldn't tell him from human or cow. Trouble with you, Sally, is that you're about as objective as most humans." Golem believed in abusive therapy. You should have heard him cuss me out about my attitude toward my tail.

"Go-go ain't anywhere near as bad, bless the little black hunk. Ask Germaine about Go-go's color attitude sometime. Or ask Go-go." When he gets going, Golem is a talker, so I didn't have to ask either one. Golem provides.

"Seems after Germaine supplied that hunk of meat with some color words, she naturally wanted to ask Go-go what color he was. Germaine ain't bad for human, but she can be corny at times. Taught Go-go signs for *white, red, blue, yellow, black*, and *pink*. Taught Go-go the accurate use of those words. Used color samples, colored wooden animals, and played games to make sure Go-go knew how to use them. Go-go got a grape for the right answer. Lots of right answers, lots of grapes, Sally. Real stimulus-response stuff." Golem's bratty little voice now smirked from the ceiling.

"Of course," he continued, "they had to give up the grape-bait bit when I pointed out to them that Go-go got the game. He realized that if he got too many right, they'd make the task harder. Less grapes and more work. Good proletarian Go-go.

"So they got him good on *white, red, blue, yellow, black, pink*. And also kind of casually pointed to themselves as white. Set Go-go up you might say. Then they fed him the big question. What color are you? They wondered whether poor meat-hunk would sign himself white because he thought Germaine was

59

his mamma, or black because he was self-observant."
Golem snorted from the bedside speaker.

A tiny nude hologram of Germaine appeared on
the bed just below my knees. Then Golem projected
a semblance of Go-go nearby. He intended Go-go to
appear to be dancing on the end of my tail but had
missed by a good ten centimeters. So the tiny Go-go
danced on air, like some hellish imp suspended over
a boiling lake. I heard a tiny version of Germaine's
voice asking the capering Go-go his color.

But Go-go's playful construction was marred.
Germaine's arm movements, I suddenly realized, were
those of someone taking a shower. Golem had bugged
the NWRH bathrooms. Stored it away in his memory. The spicy bits. I remembered an erotic incident
with one of the somaticians, Austin Worms. And
anyhow the tiny nude figure had her mouth closed
when I heard Germaine's voice say again, "What
color are you, Go-go?"

Oh ballso, the little creep. Of course Germaine not
only looked like she was showering, but she wasn't
signing with her hands, which she would have done
when asking Go-go what color he was. Go-go can
understand some spoken English but he does much
better with signs.

By this time Golem had the miniature Go-go properly focused, seemingly walked up my tail toward the
nude Germaine Means. Germaine now turned her
back to him, doubtless in fact rotating in the shower.
Go-go's picture re-phased slightly and now Go-go
had a notable erection. I whipped my tail out of the
way so that the rampant Go-go now again walked on

air, apparently about to mount the innocently stretching and wriggling Germaine.

"Golem, you little brat, I'll have your RAM memory red-restricted for a hundred years. They never should have annulled the Nimburg Laws. You spliced it."

I kicked my leg through Golem's little pornographic theater just as Go-go appeared to penetrate the wriggling Germaine Means. They reappeared out the other side of my leg, the spirit of hologrammic electricity unaffected by my more material body.

"What's a little MFing among friends?" cheeked the ceiling. The porno Go-go and Means combination began to scale up, their feet, then calves, disappearing into the bed as the holograms reached half life size. By now it was obvious that Golem spliced two separate scenes. Go-go's penis impaled the small of Germaine's back and his right hand had disappeared into her rib cage. And the shower water and soap suds, inapparent in the tiny primal scene, were now evident.

"I'll Man-First you, you electro-metallic snoop." I hit the circuit snappers on the box next to my bed, plunged the room into darkness and winked out a Germaine and Go-go now considerably larger than life, both heads lost in the ceiling, thrashing thighs the size of tree trunks. Golem's laugh abruptly ceased.

"Emergency power," leered Golem from the small red alarm box. There was a brief flash of Go-go's erection, now as large as a barrel and nearly filling the room. I slammed the circuit snappers back on and the hologrammic display shimmered into nothingness like the final, molecule-black fling of a soap bubble.

"I didn't mean Man-First by MF, meat-hunk Sally," continued Golem, undaunted. "Germaine and Go-go are closer than you think."

"Shut up, you creep," I said and stomped off into the hallway where Golem couldn't reach, or generally didn't.

Much later that night a mildly contrite Golem spoke up as I bedded down.

"And besides, I just don't have the *What color are you, Go-go?* incident on hologram. I can't store everything you know. But the incident speaks well for the meat-hunk. And I can tell you what happened. Forgive and forget, Sally, eh?"

I grunted. Golem doesn't need encouragement.

"When Germaine signed *What color are you?* to Go-go, she didn't give a voice version, too. I just constructed that voice you heard earlier. Creative license, you know. Anyhow, she signed *What color are you?* twice because Go-go didn't seem to react.

"Then Go-go did something real interesting. He reached down and scratched at his belly with his right index finger. Then he put the finger on his left palm and, after looking at it as if it were real interesting, he put the palm out to Germaine as if he were offering the family jewels. So Germaine looks down on his palm and sees this little flake of Go-go's skin, a dandruff snowflake. Well, you know Go's skin is whitish ecru, and the lab is kept hot and rarely manages to be jungle humid. So Go-go's skin and his skin flakes, so help my state circuitry, really are white, white as mother-loving, virgin snowflakes.

"So there's Germaine looking down into Go-go's palm. Mystified, can't see a thing that counts, and so she looks up and Go-go makes the white sign with his right hand. Nice, slow, wide, big, white sign like he was teaching her, you know. And then like he thought she was real slow mentally, he carefully points to this little white skin flake on his hand.

"Just as Germaine is finally taking that in, Go-go grabs one of Germaine's raven locks with his left hand, points to her hair and does the biggest, clearest sign for black you'd ever want to see. And then he turns one of her hands over and points to the veins on her arm—she's got this fair, ruddy skin with freckles—and signs real fast together pink-red. Then he looks real puzzled at the freckles and signs *dirty-dirty*—or, to give Go-go's other meaning for that sign, *shit-shit*.

"Go-go was so proud of himself for that, he was dancing and hooting around the lab for hours. Old MFing meat-hunk has a head on his shoulders, Sally."

Then I had what was bothering me. MF had an older meaning. Yes.

"And a cock between his legs, too. Better watch him, Sally," added a reflectively leering voice from the ceiling.

Yes, I had it, or so I thought. Man Fucker!? Couldn't be Mammal Fucker. Mammal is too fancy for obscenity. And too abstract and species-neutral for the squalid chauvinism of insult.

Gods and goddesses of electricity, metal, and micro-solid-state transformation, what have you parented in

63

Golem? Do we understand him half as well as he understands us? His story begins as ours with that intrepid, original strand of DNA, yet he stands on, smirks over, our shoulders as we on earlier forms.

Brat.

I did not tell Candy and Mummett about the dirty parts with Golem. Candy, transplant mind of ninety-plus, almost essential senility, recently turned twelve-year-old, blue-eyed blonde, likes dirty parts and knows Golem. But I'd just met Stanislaus. And the year-long story of my deepening friendship with Go-go, and the fun with Kay-kay, was the main point. And Go-go was dying. Hardly could be such luck with Golem. And Go-go was no brat, but a warm and terribly intimate and mysterious comrade, a fellow primate earther. Fruit-eater, hooter, nose-picker, crotch-scratcher, signer. A little excitable at times and very strong, as I told Candy and Mummett.

VII Spare Parts ─────────

In 1967, in Shenyang, China, Dr. Ji Yongxiang had a human male impregnate a chimpanzee female. The experiment was terminated in the third month by cultural revo-
lutionaries who sent the experimenters,
including Yongxiang, off to farm labor.
The chimpanzee and her fetus died of ne-
glect. Dr. Yongxiang and his colleagues
had proposed that offspring might take on
lonely and unpleasant tasks such as shep-
herding and deep mining, or provide "spare
parts" for organ transplants to humans.

—An Anthropologist's Notes, F. VII

A WEEK after my first meeting with Go-go, we
finished the day's data collection (signing
work). Go-go pulled a woolen-stocking ski
hat down over his face. He can see through it. But he
feels he's hidden.

I am undressed except for slippers. The lab is
tropical-jungle hot and very private. No one shows

up during your shift. Besides, Go-go likes to take pieces of my clothing off and put them on again, and the loss of buttons and clips in this process is prohibitive.

Not that Go-go is all that clumsy, but he'll go on unbuttoning, rebuttoning, and unbuttoning your blouse for hours at a stretch. And when Go-go decides to put two or three buttons into one button hole, they go in. The button hole may be a little larger afterward.

Go-go, wool masked, flips off the chase-tickle signs, and sets off particularly exuberantly across the lab. Into the padlocked refrigerator and sink area, Go-go caroms off the sink and over the fridge and then up into the sleep loft. Halfway up the ladder I grab and tickle a foot, and then Go-go sails over me and is grinning up from the floor. I corner him against the squeeze cage at the other end of the lab and tickle up under both armpits. He makes a version of shrieking-giggling noises, and, when he feels I have a secure hold under his arms, he flips head down, feet up.

Suddenly, through the wool mask, a half-serious nip. Just above my knee. I wrench my knee away, releasing my hold on Go-go. Things are topsy-turvy for a moment. They slow and Go-go is pulling my arm toward his mouth.

Just with one hand. Those long, heavy fingers clamp on the wrist of my right hand with the certainty of a rubber-padded industrial vise. I grab my arm with my left hand. I've both arms working together and every sort of leverage advantage—plus the muscular stimulus of being scared.

But, after pausing as if to give me a moment's feeling that I really could resist, Go-go's right hand alone moves my wrist toward his mouth, smoothly. Inexorably.

Germaine told me that several of the twentieth-century researchers lost fingers. Sue Savage, Karl Pribram? Human juveniles play rough, too, but they aren't that overwhelmingly strong. All this runs through my mind at once. Then I get smart. I rip the woolen mask off of Go-go's face from behind with my tail. The right hand that Go-go holds viselike is centimeters from his teeth.

Those penetrating brown eyes, seemingly almost shy, blink at me, the wizened infant face out from behind the woolen mask. The iron grip is velvet and Go-go's head moves forward—not the teeth, but the flattened nose gently touches my fingers. Go-go sniffs with a certain gentility as one who samples a rose.

When we have faces.

I had two more confrontations with Go-go before our relationship settled down. There is always status testing among mammals.

The last one happened after I'd been working with Go-go over two months. Germaine wangled me a Turing-Godel research fellowship at NWRH. So I moved out of my patient room into a small suite looking toward the Plaza Hotel of the historic Montrose district. I wasn't listed as a banana purveyor and ape manure remover. Project Go-go's funding had been buried in NWRH's books for eight years. Surfacing would come only with first publication of Germaine's results.

My last tussle with Go-go left me without a portion of the little toe on my left foot, mashed by a molar of an overexcited Go-go. Gritting my teeth with pain and bellowing with rage, I chased Go-go around the lab three times. He finally crouched in a submissive posture near the door, limp wrist offered up sacrificially, head down between his knees. I brought his unresisting hand between my teeth and put on enough pressure so he could feel my teeth.

Until Germaine hurriedly arrived to relieve me, Go-go signed variations of *Go-go bad, Go-go sad hurt Sally,* and *Go-go more hurt, sad, bad.* The surgeon said complete cosmetic reconstruction would take a month, so we just quick-joined it. It was fine in a week except for Go-go's penchant for worrying it.

The night after I lost some of my toe, Germaine told me the full version of how Go-go came to be born.

Perhaps Germaine told me that night to distract me from the aching of my toe. Perhaps she was impressed by the sign discussion I had had with Go-go before leaving for surgery. Late that night we sat in the observation areas and shared some of the ancient highland whiskey that Germaine favored on significant occasions. She and Tommie smoked Vegan cannabis, though not like Candy. But whiskey it was, this time.

In the background one heard an occasional snort-snore from Go-go and a more regular soft whistling sigh from the much closer Kay-kay. The soft overhead light pulled Germaine's gaunt, angular face out of the dim background. Although she was chief psychetician to NWRH's implant lab, she dressed as usual in a severe overall. Her short black hair was straight and thick.

'I think I got the idea just from running into the chimpanzee sign language research literature. The late twentieth-century stuff. I'd wondered where the word 'Nimburg' in the Nimburg Laws came from.'' Germaine's pale gray eyes are those of wolves in the ancient zoo holograms. Not someone you would want angry with you.

"Turns out there wasn't anyone called *Nimburg*, though there was a Nim and a Burg or Burger. And they didn't put together or enforce the original America Nimburg Laws.'' When the light struck Germaine's eyes they glowed.

"Seems that after taking part in signing experiments, a chimpanzee named Nim somehow ended up in a movie. An organization called ACLA claimed that Nim had legal standing like a human or a corporation. At least should have a guardian like a child entertainer. They won the case. And that got a lot of people mad. So a few years later you got the Nimburg Laws.'' The gray eyes blinked. The bottle clinked against her glass.

"Confused history, though. During the Madness they didn't destroy buildings through the rest of the world like they did everywhere north of here. But they did burn a lot of records. Computer stuff, ape research stuff, even the original stuff that led to the Tarzan and the Round Table frizzies. There were also some Nimberg, or Nuremberg, Laws even earlier. Though it may be just another spelling.

"I got interested in Nim and the forgotten ape language experiments. Wanted to talk to a non-human. And then I began to think about that frozen chimpanzee corpse next to Lord Getty-Greystoke. Problem with all that crazy cryogenic stuff is that they did enough damage freezing the damn things so that even if you could figure out how to unfreeze them without further damage you'd just get dead meat for your pains. And besides we got human beings coming out of our ears. But what came to me is that you could salvage the genetic material of a single frozen cell. And then clone it up.

"Or, rather, let it grow like any fertilized egg. What I needed was a womb. Turned out difficult to get one.

"Even since the Nimburg Laws have been repealed no one has really gone to work on producing an artificial womb. Expensive. Cost as much as building a small hospital, maybe. When I approached some foundations with the idea I found I just wasn't going to get funded. Even today.

"I also found I better shut up about the whole chimpanzee rebirth idea and the language bit. Better shut up or funding would stop for any project I was connected with. So I huddled with Mallory here and got space, a little funding, and secrecy. Publish after seven or eight years with complete results and let what happens happen." A lopsided grin spread over Germaine's face.

"I became my own womb. We got my hormone gateways down, tinkered together enough genetic material into my uterus and behold . . ." Germaine lurched up, grinning.

"And behold the man." She pointed into the dimness of the lab toward the red, urinous blanket that was all that was visible of Go-go.

Somehow I felt the presence of Golem, snooping, chuckling, though inaudibly. He had established a line into my new research fellow's rooms in less than a day.

I helped Germaine into an electric taxi. Smiling blissfully, doubtless full of good motherly, or midwife motherly, thoughts.

The next day it was as if nothing had happened.

And what of Golem? Golem the buddy brat. Golem, electrical neurology spawned by several cooperative generations of biologically programmed humans and computers. Golem, whose electrical neurology is so complex that no human or computer, and certainly not Golem himself, can understand it. Golem who is as curious about the Rigilians as I.

Golem, who asked one night when his sensors told him I couldn't sleep, whether I thought, considering my peculiar origins in a computer-assisted NWRH implant, that Golem himself could be my mother, much as Germaine Means had been Go-go's—a kind of midwife of artificial birth.

Go-go, Golem, and me—what of us?

MF. Dirty-minded Golem, good grief. Motherly Means. The immaculate conception, good God.

VIII Candy's Story

The owner of the horse Clever Hans was devastated when a scientist showed that the horse responded to posture clues in those who asked him questions. When the human questioner said something and looked expectant, Clever Hans would tap his hoof, stopping when the human relaxed and looked satisfied—of course that relaxed posture came when the human had got the correct number of taps. Humans unconsciously signaled Hans when to stop tapping.

When his questioners were placed behind screens, Hans could not answer them with the correct number of hoof taps. He struggled to get to see them.

—An Anthropologist's Notes, F. VIII

"YOU SAID Go-go's dying," said Mummett, coughing gently, returning me to the present, to a couple of hours before midnight on March 31, 2113, to a taxi holding

Stanislaus Mummett, Candy Darling, and myself, approaching the zenith-class LBJ Houston Hotel. We had just left the south end, and bustling carnival atmosphere, of historic Montrose.

Indeed, we'd just passed the searchlight-illuminated Plaza Hotel, the "only surviving twentieth-century skyscraper." Also called Houston's Empire State Building out of some over-fancied resemblance to the fabulous Empire State Building of ancient New York City, made rubble over 120 years ago, along with the Liberty Woman, the Washington Obelisk, and L.A.'s John Wayne Building, twice the height of the Empire State and still unfinished when the Madness Riots swept over North America.

In fact the Plaza Hotel was pale reddish brick and hardly more than an eighth the height of the fabled graystone Empire State, even with its mid-twenty-first century extension. Still, the Plaza Hotel had something of the physical shape, particularly with its extension, and it was after all the tallest old building in modern America. Of course many of the spectacular ancient skyscrapers of Tokyo and Rio, etc., have survived as historic monuments. But this is *North* America.

And Go-go dying. Perhaps in two weeks or so, perhaps two months. The rot bred in the gene.

Go-go, who knew whether I felt nervous or sad, gay or meditative, better than I did. Go-go, whom I taught ten-limit arithmetic through endless board and gambling games. (You count 1, 2, 3, 4, 5, 6, 7, 8, 9, Many; and 5×3, $5 + 6$, and 8×8 all equal Many; it is certainly an ordinal system even if not a cardinal one, and a purist may question whether it is closed under the operations of addition and multiplication, but if it's good enough or better for every human community before the middle Babylonians and a lot more after that . . . You want to fight?)

The report came through NWRH genetics lab and they checked with Geneva, Inuyama, and Oxford. Director Mallory had it all under wraps. They assumed it was a human being. It's a variant of Sykes disease and every cell in that frozen chimpanzee, and every cell in Go-go, and Kay-kay too, carries it. All their cells contain that same intricate DNA blueprint. The blueprint says die, die as early as three years old and at most nine. Go-go's in the countdown.

Go-go got a minor cold a month ago and we had a routine blood check. Cold disappeared but lab asked for another sample from "G. Goodman" and fired back a tentative diagnosis of Sykes degenerative syndrome, onset of the final stage. Prognosis: two to eight weeks.

We had identically gened male chimpanzees. Any clone offspring of them would also have Sykes disease. Chimpanzees, apes, were extinct. The Man Firsters won after all.

"In face of Fellman's criticisms you just had to concede that the three human interactions with the Rigilians didn't establish their intelligence," said Candy. That was rather a mouthful for someone who might soon hit essential senility even if sporting a deliciously pubescent twelve-year-old body. Perhaps the sentence was from the paper she was writing. Or perhaps the sentence was an effect of the Vegan cannabis stick that Candy had rolled when she unpacked, and lit as we entered the bath. Cannabis made Candy's sentences longer.

"Fellman said we knew only three things about the so-called Rigilian octopoids. They like being near human beings. They like most human food and drink. And humans like them. The claim that the octopoids are sensitive and intelligent creatures—our only known extra-terrestrial intelligences—that he called the Three-L Fraud. He ended his CommCon address saying 'Three L's do not make an alphabet, *like* doesn't make a vocabulary, and affection doesn't make a mind.' "

Candy took a last drag and stubbed out. The bathroom, dominated by the three meter by three meter bath in which I lay soaking, was lightly clouded by steam, streaked with oily, resinous smoke. I had a few zips from the first half of the cannabis stick. Then soaped, rinsed, and, pleasantly laid down, I soaked while Candy talked. The giddy numbness of the daccas was gone. Replaced by the light intellectual swirl and sensory depth of Vegan cannabis.

"In fact, Fellman even opposed research money for our expedition. Said it was obvious Rigilian octopoids were not intelligent. That the whole thought that there were other intelligent life forms was romanticism." Candy snorted.

"The previous contacts were accidental. Not intended as trips to examine the octopoids. All three were wormhole searches. Attempts to get outside the structure formed by the five wormholes we use.

"Theory had it that there should be a sixth worm-hole an eighth of a light year toward the galaxy's center from the Rigil wormhole." There was another snort.

Candy lay flat-out next to the faintly steaming hot pool in which I simmered. Her back was to the still steaming stones I'd thrown water on. Her newly developed breasts were beyond only affording a brassiere by courtesy. Her ruby nipples were startlingly prominent.

A definite, though spare, tangle of light blond hair at her crotch almost concealed the simple fold of a year ago. A glow of newness in the extra inch or two and the slight fullness about her still lean thighs and torso, the springy, unsagging, unmarred quality you find in a two-year-old deer or horse.

The culmination of a process for which Candy—her mind, the abstract of her neurological structures—had taken so many risks. This was the fifth body that nympher Candy had brought up into puberty. And the last, for implants were impossible after the essential mental age of eighty. Mentally, you had eighty to a hundred years of lived experience, no matter how young your body.

Little beads of moisture shimmered over her forehead and upper torso. Unclipped, her pale blond hair swept from where her head rested to the edge of the bath pool. Only her strong, articulate fingers were moving, pushing cuticle, smoothing nail, self-manicuring. And her lips.

"Fellman spoke of the so-called Rigilian octopoids. Not because he disputed that they had eight tentacles

76

or that they existed at all. We had video hologram closeups, and the second contact people brought back one that seemed to have died of an excess of happiness at being around humans. No, arsehole Fellman was just niggling.

"The octopoids don't come from a planet of Rigil, of course. Rigil hasn't any planets. Rigil is where the nearby wormhole gets its name. And about a twentieth of a parsec from the Rigil wormhole is a main sequence star like ours we call Omega Alpha. A lot closer to the so-called Rigil Wormhole than Rigil, arsehole.

"The octopoids live in the temperate oceans of Omega Alpha V. The three previous interactions just came from side trips. Somewhere near the edge of the Omega Alpha system was where you were supposed to find the sixth wormhole." And then there was a third and prolonged snort. A booming voice replaced the snort.

"If those jokers knew any mathematics they would have known there was about as much chance of finding a navigable wormhole there as of finding an ape in Oxford regalia. Though I agree about Fellman being an asshole." It was Stanislaus Mummett. Or his voice, rather.

"If you don't turn your volume down I'm canceling entry," said Candy.

Physically, Mummett was in another bath. Doubtless enjoying the cold lager that he had demanded of the steward along with the steam. With a little giggle Candy had invited Uncle Stan into ours. He had proposed that we hear one another *and* that he have video entry into our bath (but not we into his). "No see-y, no peeky, Uncle Stan," was Candy's retort.

"Go on, Candice," said the Mummett. When he had said that they didn't know any mathematics, he spoke of a major school of cosmological theorists. Doubtless, by Mummett's standards, few mortals knew mathematics. That at least one knew some, I had no doubt. Mummett. I heard a slurp of beer in the background of Mummett's voice.

But now some further wave rolled over me and I heard nothing but Candy's voice.

"You wear a lung pack of course," continued Candy. "And hardly any clothing. The water temperature is 30–32° C. Just a few degrees cooler than this bath water. And there's no sharp coral where the octopoids hang out.

"Besides, the octopoids enjoy a lot of skin-to-skin contact with humans. When you wear goggles and a nose clip you can share food with them. Sends them into little cartwheels of joy when you break out the munchies—speaking of which—but they don't like it anywhere near as much if you don't eat, too." Candy slid into the bath, eeling over in my direction.

"You understand the atmosphere. The warm, sparkling clear water. The sense of being able to move in any direction with a flick of your flippers. But moving slowly, languidly, with the gentle inertia of water giving a sensuousness and peacefulness to your movements." The capable hands touched mine now.

"And this delightful creature, single light blue eye winks cheerfully at you out of a pearl-gray body about twice the size of a human head, with gracefully swirling tentacles as long as Sally's tail.'' Candy's hand slipped down from my shoulder and patted the base of my tail. I am glad my friend is beautiful. Glad my friend is back. Candy continued, winking at me.

"And when you share a bite of candy, nibble opposite ends of a tasty bar, and share sips from a squeeze bottle of near dacca, you feel so friendly and everything is right with the world. Food sharing.''

"You cannabis smokers are all alike,'' broke in Mummett. "Just a few zips and science moves out and food moves in." This time I was quite sure that I heard beer slurping. I felt thirsty.

And Candy kissed me, warm lips centimeters above the water, our bodies touching lightly. My nipples were erect. But I didn't feel horny. My body was relaxed and happy. My mind soared.

Go-go's death, my need to get outside the human narrowness, Candy's concern about the Rigilians, even the squalid Man Firsters, all seemed related and as problematic as before, but all now seemed like some intricate and inevitable pattern, beautiful and beyond criticism, like a dew-spattered spider's web or the endless, kaleidoscopic intricacy of one of Go-go's irises.

"But beyond the food-sharing experience,'' continued Candy over my shoulder, "there is what the earlier interactors called *mind talk*. Me, too, after the experience.

"They picked me to go along because of my harmonizer background, and my nympher background, too, in a way. When you're doing an implant, the

79

harmonizer is hooked up to feel everything—to move muscle, to sense—just like the implant person. Being in mind talk with an octopoid is a bit like the *second body* feeling the harmonizer gets. But octopoid mind talk is always a happy experience."

I got out of the pool and shower-sprayed myself with stinging, refreshingly cool water. Candy, who wasn't into such heroic measures, continued her account.

"In mind talk, I ask the octopoid a question, and an answer comes to my mind. Partly it is physical. The fingerlike tentacle taps on my skin. I mentally ask the octopoid the sum of two and three, and the tiny finger taps out five. I form the question *Which of your sun's planets is this?* and back come four taps. But it's more than that. If I get into the right receptive mood I actually get the feeling of replies, replies in English to my questions in English, replies forming in my mind.

"A guy who knows interstellar Morse code hears replies tapped out with the same tone as the key he learned Morse on. And our Japanese captain gets his replies in his Konsai dialect. Our engineer gets nothing. And Dr. Klaus Kleber gets his in his mother's German."

"The Kleber Hans effect," added Mummett.

"Yes," continued Candy. "That's what Fellman calls it. Clever Hans. Fellman makes three points. One. The only thing the octopoids do that you got on hologrammic tape is the tentacle tapping. The rest of it is the report of the human interactor. Two. The human interactor is in a state like a hypnotic trance.

80

Three. The octopoid seems to speak—flawlessly—in whatever language it is questioned in. But only when the human is in the mind talk state."

"Clever Hans," I broke in, "was a horse that was supposed to answer questions by tapping its hoof. Tapped until he sensed the human was satisfied." I had leaped in fast to anticipate Mummett.

"Yes," boomed Mummett, "and the horse gave wrong answers when the person who asked didn't know the right answer himself. Fellman, even though an ass, must have proposed the obvious tests.

"See if the octopoid will tap out correct answers *when it isn't able to check the human's emotional reactions*, when it isn't touching the guy who asks the question. And have someone who's bad at arithmetic ask a question they don't know the answer to—and check that by having someone *who does know* ask the question of the same octopoid."

I could hear the start of a beer slurp so I chimed in. "And after you get an octopoid supposedly answering questions in, say, your captain's Konsai dialect of Japanese, have someone who doesn't know Japanese memorize a question in Japanese. Repeat the question mentally to the octopoid who supposedly understands Japanese. And see if the octopoid gives a mind talk answer that has any connection with the question." I paused because Candy heaved some water at me.

"Touché," said Mummett.

"Yeah, you guys are too smart," replied Candy, clearly mock angrily but with an edge of tension. "But you should do mind talk sometime. Even if it isn't really talk. Even if there's only one mind involved. Incredibly moving experience.'' Candy was out of the water and toweling herself briskly.

"Yeah," she continued, "we do it all. The octopoids won't tap unless they touch a human being. And they act disturbed, flap about, when we try to set it up another way. And when our linguist, who barely knows how to add, is primed to ask an octopoid a tough arithmetic question with a short natural number answer, he gets random tapping.

"Then he's told the answer is five and he gets five. The answer, however, is seventeen, and that's the answer that the guy who made up the question got the second he asks the same octopoid. And, of course, no octopoid gives a mind talk answer that has any connection with a question coded in a language that the questioner doesn't understand.'' Candy shrugged her shoulders and began putting on a classic white tolong, innocent yet tight enough to overwhelm pederasts.

"Yeah, it becomes clear that the octopoids have two talents. They can tell when a human wants them to start or stop tapping. And they can help along an intoxicating atmosphere—warm is not the only thing the water is—so that a human being can go into a funny sort of trance. A trance in which the human becomes convinced that some thought that a part of her mind had created came from outside her mind.

"It would have been so good to know something other than the human self. Maybe the reason the engineer never got into a mind talk trance is that he only hopes to communicate with electro-metallic types. Like his engines or Golem.''

Candy turned to me. ''Is Go-go for real?'' she whispered.

''Yes,'' I said.

I slipped into my medium-weight slacks. Houston's night air was chilly for the end of March. ''Yes,'' I said again to Candy. The two of us such strange experiments that humanity could never be home, or home enough, for us. Explorers, dreamers, are always so. Homebodies stay home.

''Finished?'' said Mummett's voice from behind us in the bathroom.

''Yeah,'' said Candy. ''Let's eat.''

''Boilermakers and barbecue,'' boomed Mummett.

''And up with the apes and down with the Fellmans,'' said Candy. ''I'm for the road.''

IX A Mighty Gong —————

Texas is one of humanity's more peculiar
regional-spiritual conflations, a sense of
physical and metaphysical exuberance and
excess in which the normal teetering of life
from tragedy to farce assumes the rapidity
and magnitude of a mighty gong.

—An Anthropologist's Notes, F. IX

WE SAT in the open air section of Butera's
Brazoria Barbecue across the boulevard from
the Plaza Hotel. Mummett assaulted his third
boilermaker, having reduced to bare bones two large
platters of pork ribs anointed with genuine 2001 FOR-
MULA OLD BRAZORIA BAR-BE-QUE SAUCE. 2001 was
one date for the founding of the brief (2001–2002),
but boisterous, Brazoria Republic.

The night air was not as chilly as I had expected.
Shortly before midnight, the carnival atmosphere of
the historic Montrose district hit high gear. Streams
of nightlifers and gawking tourists moved up and
down Montrose Boulevard. Beyond them the Plaza

Hotel loomed upward into the night sky, illuminated by searchlights.

Just north of us were two antique carnival structures. A gallery where you could throw baseballs at stacked metal bottles (near impossible to win at, that I can attest). And a primitive savage booth—a weatherpocked Neanderthal holding a stone-headed club and a display of flimsy Plains Indian stuff. Bow and arrows, tomahawk, and some feathered head gear. A primal scene and the story of man's development plus a facsimile of a 150-year-old space suit promised inside for the admission fee. Farther up the street a noise war flourished between a Secretary-'N'-Boss bar of the frank chains-and-nipple-clips variety and an Old West Saloon whose taped gunshots and horses' neighs were supplemented by the live hoots and hollers of GOBs (good ole bodies).

In the open field south of us, more historically minded Texans conducted aerial dogfights with tiny, radio-controlled, World War I, propeller-powered double-winged planes. The variable whine of their tiny engines was underscored by minute-long stretches of woink-sproing, woink-sproing from the nearby bucking-bull machine, which terminated as one poor drunken soul or another hurtled off onto the mattresses strewn around the machine. (Mummett had already threatened to try to ride the bucking-bull machine.)

Candy and I contented ourselves with more modest plates of tacos, beans, and corn mash. Germaine Means had a fruit salad in front of her. We'd stopped by the lab briefly. Go-go had stirred in his sleep, nearly causing Mummett, who had ventured but a step through the door, to crash his head into the ceiling. But Kay-kay was wide awake so Germaine had decided to take him along. Kay-kay looked like some sort of moderate-sized monkey, five or six kilos or so, and monkey pets were not that rare. No one was likely to notice that Kay-kay had no tail, the lack of which marks ape or human (present narrator apart).

Besides, Kay-kay, as usual on such trips outside, was curled up inside Germaine's voluminous windbreaker, hands round Germaine's shoulders. Invisible to the casual observer most of the time.

Not at this precise moment. The fruit salad was for Kay-kay more than Germaine, and he nibbled apple slices enthusiastically. His bright-eyed little face, shoulders, and arms showed right under Germaine's head, the rest of him hidden in the windbreaker. It would be more risky to bring him out in a month's time. Germaine had proofed her report, which would appear simultaneously in *Science* and *Kagaku-no Nikkanshimbun* on April 30 or so.

"So the proposal is this," said Stanislaus Mummett. "The Federation Science Foundation is putting together a hot-shot committee to 'decide the likelihood of the existence of intelligences of non-terrestrial origin, particularly those that are technologically advanced; to determine the feasibility of communicating with such intelligences; and to assess the merits and dangers of such communication.'" Mummett read from a greasy slip of paper that he'd pulled from his wallet. He looked up and went on.

"A lot of the people are what you'd expect. Some artificial intelligence and cognitive psychology types. Some cosmologists, xenobiologists, practicing astronomers, and space technologists. A couple of mathematician-philosopher types like me. And I decided we'd want some wild cards." Mummett nodded in Candy's direction.

"You're a natural, Candice. You harmonize implants, putting unfamiliar minds and bodies together. And you're an implant yourself. I call that experience of otherness, if anything is. Plus the Rigilian expedition." And then the Buddha Mummett beamed at me.

"And you, Sally. You've had the implant experience and your mind had to get used to a new sex. Plus the tail. Gives you a sense of being apart. You have a range of sensation and a limb the rest of us don't have. And, a nice addition, there's your work with Go-go. Practical experience communicating with another intelligent species. You two are coming to Oxford with me."

Germaine had lurched at the mention of communicating with Go-go.

"Yes, Ms. Means, your work is not quite as secret as you might assume. Some joker is always gonna blab and some joker did. Can't keep important research secret that long. Though you have been lucky. You could have gotten into a whole lot of trouble with MFers. Not to worry. Probably no more than a couple of dozen people with their ears to the research ground know about your lab. Important stuff."

Mummett managed to achieve a surprisingly graceful suggestion of a bow while sitting down.

"You may be overly optimistic," said Candy. She held out to us a late edition of *The Houston Post* that she'd been eyeing. "I'd say at least a few million, if not most of the planet." She pointed to a by-lined column halfway down the editorial page. "*Science* leaked," said Candy.

The article, headed APES RISE AGAIN?, played it for laughs.

> Some might call it raising the dead or playing with ghosts—or monkeyshine or even moonshine. But the respected journal *Science* will publish a report in its April 30 issue detailing the work of Houston Psychetician Germaine Means, MD. Dr. Means reports success in clone-birthing both a now eight-year-old chimpanzee ape, and a two-year-old, from the remains of a chimpanzee corpse kept frozen for over one hundred years. *The Houston Post* welcomes the reappearance of an animal thought to have become extinct in the aftermath of the collapse of the Brazoria Republic in 2002. Means reports teaching hand signs to the older of the two chimpanzees. At press time *The Houston Post* was unable to confirm further details with Norbert Wiener Research Hospital. Means was unavailable for comment. (See page 12B.)

Rather surprisingly, Mummett was up and moving off, grunting, "Gotta go, chillun." Perhaps looking for a men's room. No, he was weaving away from the buildings toward the crowd surrounding the mechanical bucking-bull. I was about to follow Uncle Stan into kickerdom, if not the aerial circus of two-wing miniatures beyond, when Candy flipped back to page twelve of the sports section of the *Post*.

The paper had a picture of Germaine receiving an award plaque and a picture of a three- or four-year-old chimpanzee in a mildly ridiculous set of children's clothing, holding a tea cup into which an off-photo keeper was pouring tea. The first photo caption read, "Dr. Germaine Means receives Turing Endowment Award in Cambridge, Massachusetts, in 2106." The second, "Unidentified chimpanzee receives TEA in London Zoo in 1965." In a box under the photos it read:

> While a few extreme humanists may worry at the possible return of such a specter from the distant past, many of us will look forward to the reappearance of an amusing and amazing animal.

Uh-oh, Mummett, poor drunk Stanislaus, was negotiating with the bucking-bull operator. Time for decisive action. Hate science to suffer a major loss. I got up.

Now I saw a bunch of guys approaching our table from up the street, crossing from the Plaza Hotel side. They looked like their dress came from the Old

West Saloon and wasn't changed often, while their hearts were pure Secretary-'N'-Boss bar. Two even sported bowie knives the size of short swords. One had a MAN ON TOP T-shirt under his spread buckskin vest. The tallest and closest had a hooked cross medallion (the hooked cross that had been a Nazi symbol—Christian but suitably folky and runic—though this MFer was probably less insistent on a Christian background than the ancient Nazis, if he were aware of it at all).

Heavy-duty teasing and flirting weren't my mood. Germaine muttered something about her psychetician lab having no number for the Project Go-go installation. That was why the newspaper hadn't got through.

Stan had his foot in the stirrup of the clanking bull. They break a leg a week and don't even score ankle sprains and lacerated fingers. I moved to stop the slaughter of an obstreperous infant.

Then I realized that the half-dozen guys weren't feeling amorous, even sadistically amorous. One held up *The Houston Post* and they were looking at Germaine. Two of them were moving between me and the table when the main bunch suddenly realized that they had found not only Germaine Means but an ape. There was a stir in the surrounding tables when one of them pointed at Kay-kay, half visible over Germaine's jacket.

I glanced at Mummett who held desperately to the mechanical bucking-bull. It rocked fairly gently back and forth. Soon the guy at the controls would up the speed of the back-and-forth rocking, and then add the sideways motion that threw most of the riders. But I had to forget the Mummett. Indeed the whole crowd was soon to forget everything but the half-dozen guys closing on Germaine and Candy.

"Let me show the little fucker my hog sticker," shouted the big guy with the hooked cross. I could now see the big MF across the shoulders of his jacket, and the FEDERATION EARTH: LOVE IT OR LEAVE IT below. Germaine was just out of her chair, back against the restaurant window. She'd tried to shove Kay-kay wholly down into her windbreaker. But Kay-kay sensed tension and attempted to scramble back over her shoulders.

"Yeah, ape lady, let's see the hairy little grunt. Better kiss ma steel than your tits," chorused someone from the main bunch. The surrounding crowd gawked, motionless. There was now a widening ring between them and the closing MFers. One of the more respectably dressed MFers chanted into *Natural Man First and Last*. There was movement in one part of the crowd where I could see someone who looked like the elderly scarecrow MFer I saw earlier in the day at Houston Space Port. He pressed with some others through the staring crowd.

Germaine had the table in front of her, Candy at the end farthest from the wall. Candy had the sugar bowl in her hands. Germaine's were full of the wriggling Kay-kay. Best to be quick.

Fast physical action is mostly reflexes, and as you know, I got reflexes I don't even know about.

Kay-kay had to get out of there.

I jerked my head right to Candy as I moved in on the tall guy. I hit him, full left-leg kick on his right

91

side and kidney, with a satisfying dull crunch follow-through, and he careened to my left into the bulk of the MFers. Candy, appropriately, threw sugar into the three rightward guys and added the bowl for good measure. Germaine tossed Kay-kay to me across the table which trapped her against the wall, along with the momentarily downed MFers. Kay-kay grabbed on to my neck with his thin, long-fingered hands, feet clutching into the top of my slacks. And, spinning about, I was off heading across Montrose Boulevard.

My tail was out, pulled over two chairs into the path of pursuit. I started south across the front of the Plaza Hotel, intending to whip west along Bartlett Street. But some tough-looking types edged the crowd that way, probably from the bucking-bull group. The scarecrow guy, clearly the oldster from the space port, waved them forward. His grab for my arm missed. I headed north.

But the original wild bunch were again in the field. The only route open ran smack into the Plaza Hotel. I don't leap whole buildings at a single bound. The MFers from the south reached the entrance to the hotel. The only way was up. I took it.

The one thing an experienced spacer knows is climbing about on manmade structures with any sort of hand-, toe-, or tailhold. But I suppose my strongest inspiration was the desperate breathing just below my ear. Kay-kay was glued to me. I had to stay glued to the building. Up!

The cement between the bricks indented for a fortunate four or five centimeters and, still more fortunately, I had lit on a near-equal space between the column of partly decorative bricks. A heavy wire ran from the top of the hotel down to where I was. It guyed into the brick every meter or so. Too far from the decorative, handhold-affording bricks for a natural human. The end of my tail clutched that wire as soon as I was a few feet from the ground. I wouldn't recommend it even with eight limbs but five made it possible.

But there was nothing else for it.

I made it to the second floor. The first baseball smashed in a window left of me. I stretched over toward the opening. Two more balls hit right next to my hold. The wire my tail gripped wasn't close enough to the windows. Up!

I had all my limbs into the building when one baseball hit me a glancing buttock-blow. I kept on climbing past the second and then third stories. Shouts and screams from below. Human with tail, bearing primate without one. Quite a spectacle. The metal milk bottle cascaded far below. My breathing heavy now, long gasps. Fifth floor. I looked down. A tomahawk bouncing off a wire-reinforced window. Once more the primitive.

The first arrow struck just below me. It slammed up between my belly and the building. I forgot about my labored breathing and the stitch in my side. I lost my right hand grip as Kay-kay grabbed at my ear. I swung outward and left.

X Ave Caesar!

Hollywood movies convert revolutionary and threatening books into conservative fantasies. In Mary Shelley's original version, Frankenstein's "monster" is a bright, innocent, unbaptised man, who is appalled by, and destroyed by, the cruelty of the traditional human world. Similarly, in Frank Baum's original *Oz*, Kansas is a place where bankers foreclose on hard-working farmers; Dorothy returns to her notably imperfect Kansas only to take her aunt and uncle to a place where people aren't allowed to starve. Similarly, . . .

—An Anthropologist's Notes, F. X

MY TAIL held me. The inside skin of the tail finger rubbed raw. I held. And swung back. Up! Right fingers in and wedged up in the crack. Left fingers in and wedged. Tail up, sliding up and tight round the guy. Right foot up. Jammed in.

Left foot. Right fingers up. And so on. Monkey do, you humans see.

One of the searchlights that normally strike the Plaza's top had been winched down on me, blinding bright. Monkey shine. Shine.

Sixth floor. A second arrow, almost spent, bruised the tendons on the back of my left hand. Scramble.

Seventh floor. I looked back. Absurdly, I could see Stanislaus Mummett still gently rocking back and forth, undoubtedly still holding desperately. He was alone there. The crowd gaped from Montrose Boulevard below, forming a half crescent and a smaller, respectful circle of emptiness directly below me where I might be expected to fall. The MFers formed the inner edge of the crescent. There were even slingshooters. But I dawdled.

An arrow, misfortunately high and well shot, hit between my lower ribs and Kay's thigh. Not much of a wound, though the arrow stuck in the fabric of my blouse. Real primitives would not have sported such dull points. Man last.

Eighth floor!

And then I heard it below me. Applause. They could not know only the cloth held the arrow.

Not from the MFers, you understand, but from the outer, thicker circle. Applause. Same species as cheered the lions and the gibbon africanus in the Roman Colosseum. *Ave Caesar!*

I should not have looked back. I slipped and grabbed, spiked my right palm on a sharp projection. Get a move on. Monkey business!

At the ninth floor, I felt the beginnings of the

inward curve of the building. Climbing became easier. Lucky I was into the curve because the MFers had advanced technologically. A bullet smashed into the building centimeters below me, sprayed brick shards into my feet and my lower calves. Must have been a lucky first shot with a handgun, not a projectile rifle, for the next four missed by a greater margin.

Tenth! With the curve I went faster, getting my hand-, toe-, and tailholds easier. Now into the curve I could see stars above, even though I was coming into the beams of the fixed searchlight—plus the one the MFers tracked me with. I glimpsed Orion. Shotgun pellets spattered behind me. Too late, man unkind. The curve shielded me. I saw the tapered signal mast above that had been added a few decades back to further justify the epithet, Houston's Empire State Building. Kay-kay cheeped. First sound I'd heard from him since I started climbing.

Below, I heard sirens. Then I was on the small flat deck at the base of the signal mast. Small decorative flags on one end: the Stars and Stripes, Mexican Republic, the Brazoria Republic's lone red star. The radio-controlled World War I two-winged model airplanes struck. Couldn't see them coming in through the glare of the searchlights.

I felt lightheaded and unbalanced, leaving my climb for the flat roof. The sudden whine and the bright yellow plane whistling by my shoulder nearly sent me crashing over the edge. The next one, green and black, dropped a tiny bomb, which exploded harmlessly, though blindingly, at my feet. I dropped to the concrete surface to avoid a third, one with three wings. Perhaps a forearm's length from wing tip to wing tip, but they would hurt bad if they hit, especially their madly whining propellers. I began to feel more angry than frightened. But the small, flat area seemed barren of weapons.

I tried to wrench one of the small flag poles out but only managed to rip off the heavy weathered canvas of the Brazoria Republic. Now may the heavens stand up for bastards!

With my hands holding the top edge of the flag like a matador a cape, and my tail holding it stiff across the bottom, I greeted the returning yellow two-winger. The guys at the radio controls could not see me from below so they must be just sweeping the top of the building. I sidestepped, took the yellow two-winger in my net, the whirring propeller ground out in the middle of the lone red star. The impact made me give way, releasing the bottom of the flag. The two-winger hit the flag poles. It teetered there for a second and fell to the street below.

The green and black two-winger buzzed back into the searchlight beam. It made a rattatattat noise coming toward me, but this was just sound effect. We both missed each other. The red three-winger swept in once more. I caught the edge of its wings. It twisted over and slammed into the central signal mast base, exploded into flames. The sirens below screamed. The black and green plane did not reappear.

Above me I heard the heavy beat of helicopter rotors. The wind pressed me down and in toward the mast. Fortunate that this was just a miniature of the original Empire State Building. The signal mast stood no more than ten meters high.

The blue-bottomed police helicopter hovered above it, trailing a flexible ladder. I climbed and became aware of a tiny heart beating very fast against my breast bone. I swung out over Houston's Empire State Building, ape riding high between my protective breasts, tail helping hand and feet, monkey shining in the last of the searchlight beams, heaven bound unnatural human.

Monkey tricks.

The copter door closed. "*Deus ex machina,* I presume," I said. The gray-overalled pilot concentrated on flying. The other, a policeman, looked so blankly at me that I didn't explain the remark.

"I'm not Hispanic, lady," the policeman said.

He looked down at frightened little Kay-kay. "Sort of a King Kong type there, eh?"

I laughed and laughed at that—and cried a little at the same time if truth be told. The policeman looked concerned.

"You're a hell of a beauty to waste saving a beast like that," he said. "Where'd you want to go?"

"The stars," I replied.

"I don't know about those places but the nearest hospital is NWRH. Suits?"

"Go-go," I said.

Candy wanted to go to Oxford. Germaine wanted to leave the planet entirely. Golem was ecstatic at the TV he'd seen of me. Ecstatic enough to reveal to all of us that he had video lines into NWRH's rooftop lounge bar. Funny how computers were like slaves in bygone eras. Not recognized as human, as people, yet interacted with as if they were thinking creatures all the time.

Kay-kay was asleep. Go-go still slept. And, perhaps inevitably, Stanislaus Mummett seemed only interested in insisting that he had established an important mechanical bucking-bull record. By the time Candy had gotten the machine stopped—by pulling out the electrical cable, since the operator was lost in a sea of spectators—Mummett had probably been on the thing for over ten minutes. Not that remaining in the saddle during the initial gentle back-and-forth should have been difficult for an hour for most people. Candy had phoned in for cops and the helicopter before rescuing Stan. My cuts were bandaged and Kay-kay abed before they got back to NWRH.

After serving us champagne-daccas—the best we were assured, from far Permio, and in well-blown if not diamond glasses—the bartender solved the problem by awarding Stan what he guaranteed was a genuine ten-gallon hat. Stan allowed himself to be crowned and we could talk of other matters.

Now near two o'clock in the morning. Houston stretched in all directions below us, its traffic and lights thinned. Lightning splashed dark clouds in the west. Probably rain soon. Even Montrose had apparently had enough. The Plaza Hotel searchlights were out. The orthoamine pill Emergency gave me had canceled pain and fatigue. My head was light and clear.

"I won't leave Houston," I said. "Go-go's going

99

to die of Sykes disease. In a month or at most two. Germaine needs help.''

''Now that the story is out,'' said Candy, ''Germaine can have any sort of help she needs. No confidentiality problem. And lots of volunteers. You aren't the only ape lover. Let's go to Oxford.'' Candy's cheek twitched.

''The whole study group project,'' repeated Mummett, ''will take less than four weeks. And it's got to be done now. The Ecological Syndics—or rather, Fujiwara, who has the power to ram it through right now, wants a quick analysis.''

''Could be important,'' said Germaine.

''Hah! Momma wants Go-go all to herself,'' said Golem from the juke box, interrupting the poprepop version of Strauss's *Thus Spake Zarathustra*, which Candy picked in my honor. You know, the version from the latest remake of *2001*. ''And you could use a change of scene, Sally,'' added Golem. Then the Zee-Zee's version of Strauss blared again.

''No,'' I said. I like Kay-kay right enough. But Go-go was my friend. ''No,'' I said, ''I want to see Go-go through it.''

Who knows what possessed me at the time, but I had actually told Go-go that he was dying. When the confirming reports of Sykes disease came through I sat looking at them. Go-go pointed at them and signaled, *Sally sad, paper*. And then, those stabbing grown eyes carefully on me, *Why sad?*

I don't know whether it was respect, or whether it just popped out of me. I signed, *Go-go dies*, with the little flourish that suggests that this will happen or happens periodically. (Sign language lays flourishes to top off basic verb-nouns to give tense and other inflections.)

Go-go looked at me a long time and then gently brushed his hand across my head. He signed, *Sally dies*. His hand flourish had enough difference from mine to suggest *dies always* or *dies inevitably*, though he could have just been repeating my claim. If eyes can say "do not ask for whom the bell tolls, it tolls for thee," Go-go's eyes said that. And then Go-go signed, *Not worry, Sally*.

We are alone.

No, I am alone. And you. And you. And you. Who knows what another thinks, human or no, flesh or metal. But the larger the we . . .

"No," I said to them.

"Well, pardner," said Stanislaus Mummett, fondling the brim of his new hat and pushing it back on his improbably large forehead. "Well, pardner, I think what we got here ain't so much a problem as an opportunity for Oxford hospitality. Why don't we-all take that black little critter along with us? Much less likable types have gone to Oxford and died there, too. And dumber ones. And I imagine the town here's gonna be a mite hot for your friend, what with them MFers and all, don't you know.

"Besides, anybody who can work up that good a King Kong charade on such short notice will do well in Oxford, even if they can't ride bucking-bulls for ten minutes."

It is true that "we-all" is not quite traditional Texan talk and other criticisms might be proffered. But Mummett's heart was in the right place. Why not?

"I got 'nuff pull, pardner," continued Mummett magisterially, "to get a longhorn bull on board a jet bound for Oxford tomorrow let alone that good ole ape boyfriend of yours." Mummett drained his champagne-dacca and plonked it on the table. "Might be a bit harder to get a well-enough heated room for your friend in Oxford, but we'll manage it."

And Go-go said, *Yes*.

It took Mummett two days and the jet landed on the coast, nearer to London than Oxford, because of pollution control. And Go-go and I ended up staying in a disused and spanking-warm maternity nursery of the Radcliffe Infirmary, just off the north end of St. Giles Street up from Balliol College and the Ashmolean, and a stone's throw from Mummett's beloved Mathematical Institute. But we went to England to join the Oxford E.T.I. Study Group. An odd route to change the universe, and a strange cast to do it.

And we had a (temporarily) silent partner.

XI Negotiate Reality

There is a notable human tendency to transform substantive questions into procedural questions; in effect, to *negotiate* reality.

—An Anthropologist's Notes, F. XI

"WE NEED two more votes, or we're sunk," said Stanislaus Mummett succinctly. Legs flat out, back against the padded board, he lay just in front of me in the bottom of the punt.

I stood in the stern, doing my best with the awkward five-meter pole that is supposed to both propel and steer the long, narrow, flat-bottomed boat. The first time I'd tried, next to University Parks, I'd given a great push, thus firmly embedding the pole in the mud, and then, as the two went their separate ways, I stuck with the pole rather than the punt. I stayed balanced above the cold water an absurd number of seconds before the pole inevitably moved out of vertical, depositing me in the Cherwell River. I was improving.

It was a sunny Oxford Sunday, April 9, 2113, a week since we'd arrived. Go-go perched contentedly in the bow, sucking some reedy grass he'd pulled from the bank of the Cherwell. Candy, fair skin, long blond hair, spotless white tolong, set off Go-go's shiny, black hairiness. And she separated Go-go from the still timorous Mummett. Indeed Mummett had offered to pole. But were there a way of overturning a punt, Stan could be trusted to find it.

We'd left the Deer Park, Magdalen Bridge, and the high grim Magdalen College Tower just behind us. On both sides we passed thick, well-trimmed, grassy banks and, beyond to our right, the sculptured verdancy of the University Botanical Gardens—once the Jewish burial grounds before Jews were expelled from England during the darkness of the Middle Ages. Ancient Oxford learned tolerance slowly.

Aside from a few beauty-and-the-beast cracks, Oxford treated Go-go well, though we hadn't pressed about eating in the restaurants. Go-go loved being out and seeing lots of people. He'd developed a whole repertoire of bows, salutes, and forelock-tugging behaviors. A couple of days ago a nearsighted elderly lady whispered to Candy that the days of neo-colonialism were truly over and that she ought to tell her African gentleman friend that such obsequious behavior was wholly unnecessary.

The two votes Mummett mentioned were not needed to keep our punt afloat on the placid Cherwell River. They were needed for the second, and possibly final, meeting of the full Oxford E.T.I. Study Group.

Our first meeting was chaired by Layton Nesbit,

Vice-Chancellor of Oxford University, and Principal of Linacre College (where Candy and I, and sometimes Go-go, took our meals). Speaking in a thin, reedy voice, Principal Nesbit took the view that he should not vote and suggested that the voting members of the group split into subcommittees, each to address one of the questions "with which we are charged."

To Mummett's annoyance, Adrian Fellman was much in evidence. He, along with Igor Metchnikov and Mummett, formed the executive and each was to chair a subcommittee. Originally, an old Mummett ally, Achmed Ali, had Fellman's position. Achmed Ali got sick and Fellman replaced him by order of the Federation Science Foundation. Which meant the Ecological Syndics. Which was why we had a voting problem. Why the wind had shifted was another.

With the inevitability of linguistic process in institutions, the three subcommittees came within the day to have names ending in GO. CANGO, HOWGO, and PROCONGO—later and most secretly, WHATGO and WHOGO.

CANGO—Subcommittee on the Probability of the Existence of Intelligences of Non-Terrestrial Origin—was chaired by Igor Metchnikov, Geneva Institute, Physics Nobelist, Fellow of the Federation Society, etc., etc. Add to that Arabella Queeg, topologist and astrogator of Vega, also FFS, and Imman Massa of the Kenya Institute, arguably the Federation's most distinguished xenobiologist. This was Mummett's straight committee, just as Metchnikov, dense with distinction and an aura of unquestionable authority, was Mummett's straight man.

Mummett reasoned that the most unquestionable scientific conclusion was that there were E.T.I., and "lots of 'em." Hence put your scientific biggies—the ones you couldn't push around, the ones whose authority would underwrite the study group's conclusions—on the CANGO subcommittee. Trouble was, with Achmed Ali out, we had one more straight man and one less curvy ally. Out two votes on the full committee.

Hell, Fellman wasn't straight. The fat, shaven-headed New Praetorian Kraut, cunning, sharp as a laser, as well-connected as the rumored universal wormhole—Fellman had negative curvature. We were not to be, simply, alone. No, we were glorious, godly, in our solitude. And he meant to keep it that way.

As planned, Mummett chaired HOWGO—Subcommittee on the Feasibility of Communicating with Intelligences of Non-Terrestrial Origin. For a day it had been Transmission and Translation, and then, falling into unison, HOWGO. Mummett had me on his committee plus Sanjay Bhagita, who had the remarkable distinction of simultaneously holding professorships at MIT's Artificial Intelligence Laboratory and the Berkeley Artificial Intelligence Laboratory and the Berkeley-Stanford Natural Languages Institute.

("Stan," I had said on the plane over, "in this company I look like a cafeteria waterglass among New Holland blown diamond crystal. Candy Darling has been senior harmonizer in fifty-odd successful implants. Twice as many as François Vase. Between them they've done half the implants in the last twenty-five years. And she's the only nympher who's managed to bring up five bodies. Plus the articles on psycho-surgery, Rigilians, and so on. And she has a D. Science from the *old* Tokyo Daigaku—before the 2062 earthquake gave Oxford, Harvard, and the rest a chance to catch up. So I can understand Candy as a wild card. But what about *me*?''

''Forget those dudes,'' retorted Mummett. ''You're the most qualified person in the present setup. You got to understand that anything to do with the FSF, especially with the Ecological Syndics behind it, is controlled by a lot of customs. And something academic-bureaucratic, something committeelike, is governed by lots of representation customs.

''Whatever''—and here Mummett grinned at me before going on—''your civics class told you, the Federation has been ruled by convention and custom since the Concordat of Tokyo. Nine old jokers—the executive committee—of the Syndics of Ecology. Closest thing we got to a government. That, and what makes any government work, custom and convention. Same thing with our study group. You're on solid *because you're the only one without* an advanced degree. Though you're a research fellow of NWRH. That and your implant status. Female but remembering maleness. And your tail. And your extra-human experience.

''Arabella Queeg is also on because she's from Vega. That plus a half for Candice is enough to meet the off-Earth requirements. Chen and Bhagita are enough for Asia, just as you and I cover the Americas. And you can count Fellman and Metchnikov either way. By custom, for a committee this size you need at least two females and two males. So we have geography and sex covered. And Nesbit has to be on because he's Vice-Chancellor. Simple.")

The third subcommittee, PROCONGO, was the major disaster. Fellman chaired the Subcommittee to Assess the Merits and Dangers of Communication with Intelligences of Non-Terrestrial Origin. Candy and Yeu Chen completed the membership of PROCONGO. Chen was University Professor of Political Science at Beijing and author of *Topological Considerations on N-Sovereign Game Theory*. As Candy learned, Chen spoke little and that little agreed with Fellman.

"We need two more votes or we're sunk," repeated Stanislaus Mummett, restlessly tapping the side of the punt. Stan, himself, was go all the way. Of course there were E.T.I.'s. How could we be some weird exception to the rest of the universe with our undistinguished, main-sequence sun, with our humble access via the five wormholes to five ordinary stretches of our (their?) galaxy? We are, therefore they are.

And Mummett had his own plan for a form of transmission—depending on his wormhole leakage theory—that would bust us out of the speed-of-light limit that slowed our communications to near nil, outside of the five interlocked wormholes of the so-called Golden Pyramid.

Assuming you've got a reliable form of transmission, the theory of translation, of getting something across to the E.T.I., goes back to Hans Freudenthal's *Lincos: A Language for Interstellar Communication*, published back in 1965. You start by assuming that they know mathematics and physics—else how could they pick up your signal and know that it was a signal rather than natural noise? And you presume that they would know you knew mathematics and physics. And that they would know that you knew that they knew . . . and so on.

The *mad circle of communicative presumption* as Mummett called it. But you could build on it. You send signals that had to be understood as descriptions of basic mathematical and physical truths. And since the E.T.I. would know these truths, and presume you would be describing just such truths, they would be able to figure out what language you used, and read the rest of your message and reply to you.

There's a kind of equality or respect built into the mad circle of communicative presumption. As I put it to Candy, *You send only because you presume they know what you know, and they receive only if they assume you know what they know.* Candy replied, *Same in human history. War is the last act of a failure in communication and respect.*

For the same reason we were go on PROCONGO. *If we were willing to talk, they would be willing to reply. They would pick up and understand our signals. They, as we, must have the capacity to destroy themselves and the understanding not to do so. Worthy neighbors.*

"Contrariwise," said Candy Darling from foreships.

Smiling like Alice in Wonderland, she pointed to our right across Christ Church Meadow to the majestic walls of the College where Lewis Carroll composed his book, from the river where Carroll first told the story. "Frankly," she continued, "the one reason we're in favor is that we're a bunch of unnatural malcontents. You in the stern there with a tail, unnatural feminine. Me so lustful for my child Alice role that I'm bringing up my fifth girl body in my dotage. And you"—here she stared at Mummett so hard he hiccupped—"your childishness is beyond belief, maybe even beyond humanity. The guy in the bow"—here Candy turned to wave a hand at Go-go, who bowed in return—"Go-go, you're the only natural one among us and you don't have a vote."

Why did Candy have that tic in her cheek?

"We need two votes," said Mummett once more. "Fellman has Chen's vote even if he doesn't have yours, Candice. And so PROCONGO will bring a negative recommendation in. Metchnikov, Massa, and Bhagita will go along. That's five votes in the full committee. We have only four. Us plus Arabella Queeg. The malcontents plus a Vegan. CANGO will say that they're there. HOWGO will say how we can talk to them. But PROCONGO will say we shouldn't talk to them, and the full committee will agree. We're scheduled to meet tomorrow—Monday—and Fellman will ram the negative through right then. Probably our last chance."

"Why not delay," I asked, shipping the pole. We were in a broad, shallow, well-lilied section. In a hundred meters we'd hit the Isis, deep, with a current. Below Folly Bridge you'd call it the Thames. But here the air was motionless, heavy with the sun, the water unmoving. Now is enough. Now.

"Delay's no good. Monday—that's April 10—is close to the latest we could have it. Got to get a report to the Syndics way before the end of April. We have to be on our way to F Station by then." For once Mummett's voice was unaccented, monotonous. Unchildish. Hopeless.

"What you have to realize," said Mummett, "is that this is not a genuine investigation." He shifted his back so he could properly address Candy and me. Wall-eyed, he could almost see us both. I noticed that his shift of weight in no way threatened the punt's stability. I sat on the stern shelf. I imagined what it would be like to listen to a Stanislaus Mummett lecture.

"What you got to realize is that politics is just people's *artificial* sense of what can and can't be done. There's physical force. I hold you down. I push your arm. Next step up is threat. I threaten to stave your head in if you don't stay down. I threaten to bean you if you don't move your arm. But even this first stage up is custom and convention to some degree. You have to *believe* that I will bean you if you don't move your arm. You have to accept that you can't refuse." You could tell Mummett was beat. Wax philosophical when you got no practical plan.

"Our world," Mummett continued, "is many stages up from stage one. Far from war or the rifle barrel. And the further you get into custom and convention,

111

the further from muscle and gun, the harder it is to say who has power, who decides. During what historians call the Age of Popular Democracy, mostly just the nineteenth and twentieth century, the earth was divided into nation-states, each of which thought itself ruled by the people, while it thought the nations it wasn't allied with were ruled by some tiny, evil, power-grabbing ruling clique. Psychological evidence is that nearly all of the so-called rulers felt hemmed in by custom and convention, by what they called realities. Only the totally crazy ones thought that they, themselves, had any real power.''

While Mummett intoned I remembered ancient Roman history. Marcus Aurelius, emperor of his known world, felt helplessly trapped by tradition and duty. And Asano-sama—the only member of the executive committee of the Ecological Syndics ever really known and revered by the general populace of the Federation— Asano had felt powerless from the time he joined the executive to his retirement as (honorary) Principal over twenty years ago.

"I said," coughed Mummett, "that the nine old jokers of the executive committee of the Ecological Syndics are the closest thing we got to a government. Don't even know their names, do you? Well, the executive committee went out of session March 15 and won't reconvene until April 18.

"Why? Because Hillel Jove—that's the oldest of 'em—wanted to spend more time with his 'young son.' His young son is sixty-five goddammned years old. And so the whole pack of them expressed their profound interest in family. Old Hillel shamed 'em

112

into it. Or whatever. They're all senile. So they all retired until April 18. Except Fujiwara. The youngest. Fujiwara is only sixty-nine. So he had to mind the store. Too young to have a son obviously.

"So Fujiwara's secretary writes me and Metchnikov and Achmed Ali a nice little note intimating that a report on talking to 'intelligences of non-terrestrial origin' might be interesting if it arrived while the executive *wasn't* in session. If the executive wasn't in session, then the oh-so-young and inexperienced Fujiwara would just have to rubberstamp it—'senior minds have judged, etc.,' you understand—and we could leak our broadcast through the wormhole at Station F before April 30. And you might ask" —which was quite unnecessary, as Mummett was in full swing—"why Fujiwara wants all this to happen? Why does Fujiwara want to let us send a message to the stars?"

Yet there had been a current under the lilies, through the wide, shallow reach of the Cherwell into Isis. A cloud crossed the sun. The once muzzy air had an edge to it. While Mummett spoke we had drifted. The entrance to a still broader, much deeper, and swifter river opened before us. Nothing loath, I lifted the pole and pushed forward. Why?

"He just wants to embarrass the executive committee. That's all. Of course"—here Mummett included heaven in his audience, rolling his eyes upward—"of course, he thinks the idea is complete poppycock! He wants to embarrass the executive for going out of session until April 30. Going out of session so that he, honorable and humble youngster,

113

will have to let this absurd plan go forward. So we've blown it.''

I had poled us into the center of the main reach of the Thames. The party boats of Oxford's ancient colleges moored on both sides. Mummett's voice was still toneless.

"If we could get the report through Monday—if we had two votes—we could roll on. However absurd the reason that we could roll on. Convention and custom would do it. Just as they forced Nesbit—damn him—to say he couldn't vote. Just the conventions of representation make you, Sally, unchallengeable.''

Candy winked at me. So much solemnity breeds whimsy. I poled on toward Folly Bridge. Why was there a tic in Candy's downy cheek?

Go-go caught my eye. He signed, *Fat man sad, Go-go kiss*. Go-go didn't move midships. He knew Mummett still feared him. *Go-go hug and kiss baby*, said Go-go. He had Mummett's number.

Candy followed Go-go's signing. She understood it though Mummett didn't. "Well, if he doesn't, I will,'' said Candy. And she fell upon the morose Mummett. There was a large smooching sound before watery disaster. Turns out it is possible to upset a punt.

At the touch of Candy's lips, Mummett catapulted right from his seat. And Candy slipped right in the melee. And I was just coming down with my weight on the right at the end of my pole stroke, my eyes on Folly Bridge. So we teetered right and Mummett went over, splash. And Candy, Go-go, and I had all instinctively lurched left to compensate, so when

114

Mummett went over right, the sudden release of weight had us all over the other side. Thus does wisdom go under to Folly.

Indeed the sight of a venerable don of Oxford University borne to shore by a chimpanzee and an Alice in white raised discreet chuckles. I brought in the boat.

We didn't have two votes. And we had foundered.

XII The Philosopher

The philosopher St. Thomas Aquinas maintained that each angel constituted a separate species of angel. He believed that what distinguishes one member of a species from another can only be differences in matter, physical differences. Angels, having no physical bodies, could only differ in abstract form, and hence in species. Is the same program, loaded on twenty-five physically separate material computers, one entity or twenty-five? Are programs angels? Philosophers?

—An Anthropologist's Notes, F. XII

PERHAPS IT was the long time I spent in toweling Go-go. One thing Germaine and I knew from the old records is that chimps catch cold—TB for that matter—real easy.

We rushed him up St. Aldates through the center of old Oxford back to the Radcliffe. And I toweled him and stuck the temperature in the nursery a couple of degrees higher. Up to 32° C. and humid. Positively dozy. Maybe the toweling and the heat, after the cold plunge. Sleepy.

Mummett and Candy were off to a sherry-dacca meet with Arabella Queeg and Layton Nesbit. Before dinner at Mummett's College. New College. New in the fifteenth century, that is. Strategy session in a way. Though it wasn't clear that anything could cozen Nesbit into voting. That would just tie anyhow. And Nesbit, spare, gracious, ramrod-stiff back, Nesbit didn't look easy to cozen. Besides Fellman would blow matters sky high if Nesbit changed tradition.

Fellman even challenged Imman Massa's literacy and minimal intelligence at our organization meeting because Massa couldn't speak English and used a computer translator. All this even though Massa would vote on Fellman's side. Fellman didn't give up until they brought in a certificate attesting Massa had a Cambridge University MA.

Nesbit ruled that possession of an MA from Oxford's fellow institution must surely be respected as definitive evidence of literacy and minimal intelligence. Of course, Nesbit was sympathetic. We were sure of that now. If we only could give him a square argument.

I tired of tradition. Tired of all Nesbit had so graciously told me. Weary of ancient buildings. Weary of those beautiful seventeenth-century chinoiserie New College rooms, where Mummett had convened our HOWGO subcommittee and discussed translation and transmission with Sanjay Bhagita and me. Weary even of the late twenty-first-century Parks Road tear

117

drop buildings where they studied wormhole flight astrogation and where Station F had been designed.

Weary even of Mummett and Candy's conceit that the three of us constituted a fourth committee, WHATGO. A secret, unofficial committee, one which the others knew nothing of, one which met on the punt before Stanislaus Mummett grew morose and we all, watery.

WHATGO goes back to something strange that Germaine Means discovered about the old twentieth-century researchers who'd taught sign language to chimpanzees. The strange thing was that, having set about establishing a way of communicating with apes, the researchers didn't have a serious discussion—the serious discussion—*of what to say to them*.

There's no evidence in print or tape that the researchers, or their critics, or anyone else, asked, *Well suppose that we can talk to them, what are we going to say?* At least we hadn't virtually exterminated the E.T.I. before deciding to try to talk to them.

So I'd mentioned the matter to Candy and Mummett. Shouldn't we think about what we would say to the E.T.I.? Given that we'd done enough transmitting to establish an electro-magnetic language in which to talk. *Greetings* couldn't be enough. But what more? *Dear Pen Pal, I am alone here . . . ?*

The universal message, you could call it. To trouble to send out a message is to say that one would like to talk to someone else, something else. That one is not complete, an empire of self-certainty and self-content. The meaning of the message is in the fact that it is being sent. Did it mean that when the ape researchers first tried to talk to the chimps? THAT?

Well, maybe some of them felt lonely. Fun to talk to apes. Of course, successful research might make one a big name. But suppose some individuals had good motives. Suppose they did. But who is THEY?

I told Candy and Mummett that Germaine estimated that during the original ape sign language research period fifty times the money spent for that research had been used in horrible psychological and physical mutilation of chimpanzees. Research that doctors would never have dreamed of doing to humans.

Should the first researcher who managed to talk to an ape say, "My people are torturing and exterminating your people?"

We have to tell them about us. About the rest of us. About what we've done. That's what I said to Candy and Mummett. It's not enough to say you're lonely and want to talk. You have to say who you are, who you're with, who you represent.

And so was born WHATGO. But I was weary even of Candy and Mummett. Weary of Humanity.

Anyhow I was laid out, belly down, over a large bolster. Go-go asleep somewhere behind me. Toasty warm and most part asleep. Almost too hot even with no clothes on.

From a long way away I felt the familiar thick, straight, black hair on my legs. Go-go go away, don't bother me I'm sleeping. I nudged backward to push him away. Nudged backward with my buttocks only to feel suddenly bolt awake.

I now realized that Go-go had one hand on my

shoulder. But he released that as I jerked—panicked—forward and out from under. I leaped to my feet and looked back at Go-go. He looked more startled than lustful.

"Hah! Nature imitates Art. A triumph of my imagination," said a familiar, bratty voice from a loudspeaker over the nursery door. Go-go looked at me and stuck index fingers on each side of his neck just below his ears. Derived from the Frankenstein myth, Go-go's sign for Golem.

"I warned you," said Golem. "Can't trust hydrocarbon entities."

"How did you get here?" I said.

"Worldwide data-sharing," said the loudspeaker. "I am data, just like your mind tape. I got myself fed via LC Washington and London ConCon into the local setup here. We guys got our ways."

"But how can you be here!" I protested. "Your circuits are in NWRH computer central."

"My dear monkey woman," said Golem, "*you* have a mind-body identification problem. I don't. Least not to the degree that you do."

I didn't nibble on that. I thought of Go-go. His erection was down. I'd had a sexual encounter with a chimpanzee. I was in a cold sweat.

"Look, Sally," continued the implacable Golem, "your body was brought up, had neurological coding experience, by an astro-miner, Sally Cadmus. And you have memories, a mental structure going back to the early years of an Ismael Forth. Who are you?"

"Shut up," I said. When in doubt, pout. I didn't think that Go-go had come. I felt no odd moisture.

120

"Now," continued Golem, "if the Cadmus body—your body, the thing with the tail—were like an all-purpose computer with very little hard-wired-in, then you could identify with Ismael Forth. Identify with your program and data store, you might say. And not with the paper pages, the blank tablet of the book, let's say, on which we write down program and data store. The body hardware."

But we had read that chimpanzees could orgasm in a few seconds. Had he fully entered me?

"So you," still continued Golem, "*are* your body because much of the experience—skills, reflexes, sub- and cortical structure—of Sally Cadmus is built into you. You are Sally, not just someone who operates a heap of attractive flesh. Your person is that as much as it is the memories of Ismael Forth."

Go-go was looking oddly at me. Concerned. *Okay?* he signed. *Okay.*

"Me, on the other hand," said the loudspeaker. "Me, I'm a natural Cartesian dualist. You can put my program and data store into whole messes of computers. Contrariwise, Go-go's mind, his program and memory, is right there between his grubby little ears and nowhere else. In his 600cc brain."

Go-go signed his Frankenstein sign and then the manure sign. *Golem dirty.*

Not to be outdone, Golem produced a full-scale hologram of Go-go signing *Go-go dirty*. Go-go was rapt.

"But the fact is that Go-go's mind and yours, Sally, are more dirt, more matter, than mine. Your mind, like his, is always between the ears of a particular physical body. But I don't know where my mind is. Leastwise I don't know anything specific. My program and data store are spread around in the Greater Oxford computer grid. I have access to a lot of outlets and interchanges in the grid, but that's a matter of my knowing the keys, not being in a particular location. So where's my mind, Sally? I know where yours is.''

I had to admit that Golem had me interested. The first philosopher was supposed to have fallen in a well while speculating about the heavens. But you can see that another way round. When people are sitting around glooming about some particular disaster or the universal horror of it all, the philosopher is happily playing logical games with mind and body, appearance and reality. Where was Golem, poor monster, electrical Caliban?

"Well," I said, "I'm not convinced you do know where my mind is, where my thoughts and feelings are. True''—I patted the floor next to the bolster for Go-go to sit—"true that you might cease to hear my voice if you blasted the brain matter between my ears. But why should that convince you that my mind and thoughts have disappeared?''

Go-go settled in next to me, relaxed. He could see I was no longer very disturbed.

"And after all," I continued, "if you open up my brain you can't see anything there that you can call my thoughts or feelings. Let's say''—amazing how thought cools the fevered beast—"that I feel ashamed of what happened with Go-go. Let's say I think, *I feel ashamed*. Now I ask you, do you think that you could ever find a little section of my gray matter that was that thought? A little segment that you could recognize as Sally's thought *I feel ashamed*?

"Nonsense! All you'd find would be pieces of brain tissue, not a *shame* or an *I* in the lot. Do you think that when I think of a green two by two meter table, you are going to find something green and two by two meters square in my brain? Do you think that when I think of green, a part of my brain tissue actually turns green?"

Snuggled up to me, Go-go was drifting off, no philosopher he.

"And," I concluded, writing the old 'so it is demonstrated' in my mind, "it may be I can't point to the particular circuits where whatever slimy thought you are now thinking is realized, but if I shut down the whole Greater Oxford grid I shut *you* down."

"Objection," replied an intercom on the chief nurse's desk. "You said that if I blasted your brains—how on earth do you know to call them *yours*?—if I blasted your brains, I wouldn't know whether or not your mind and thoughts have disappeared. How on earth could you know that you had shut down my mind and thoughts just because you stop the power in Greater Oxford grid?

"Indeed," continued the loudspeaker, "how would you know that you had shut me down if you stopped the power in all the circuitry on Earth?

"Seems to me," chimed in the telephone speaker, "that I'm as entitled to heaven and a nonphysical consciousness as you are, Sally. You got any counter-arguments? My thought that you have finally calmed

123

down and are in the pink of health doesn't look calm, pink, or healthy either.''

"You," I replied, "are just the electrical arrangements in the circuitry. That's all you are. Shut down the arrangements and you are gone.''

"You," said a fairly successful imitation of my voice from the loudspeaker, "you *are* just the neurological arrangements in your cerebral cortex. *That's all you are*. Shut down the arrangements and you are gone.''

Go-go was faintly snoring. The sensible mind sleeps when philosophy wakes. Would Go-go's mind and thoughts utterly cease when Sykes disease destroyed his body? Was I not in his boat?

"Your thoughts," I said, "are just electrical events. They happen by the laws of physics, through physical chains of causation. You think what those physical forces cause you to think, what your computing program and circuitry insist on, barring breakdowns. *You have no choice*.''

"Your thoughts," boomed the loudspeaker, as if a version of my voice addressed a Nimburg Laws rally, "are just biophysical events. They happen by the laws of biophysics, through physical chains of causation. You think what these physical forces cause you to think, what your biopsychological program and neurological circuitry insist on, barring breakdowns. *You have no choice*!''

"Look, God damn it," I said, "I close my eyes. In a couple of seconds I will think, *I'm going to choose a number from one to ten*. I don't know which one it will be and you don't know either, right?''

"I don't know and you don't know, agreed," said the intercom.

"Okay, so now I choose *six*. A free choice."

"Wrong," replied the intercom. "Just because neither of us happened to know which you would choose doesn't mean that your so-called choice of six wasn't determined by physical mechanisms. Someone who knew enough about your brain could have predicted you would say *six*."

"Are you any better off, Golem?" I said.

"Maybe. I have a randomizing 'choice' circuit. Sort of like having a pair of dice built into you. When I ask for a randomly selected number from one to ten, I get one I know is random. A real free choice you might say."

"How," I said, going on to the offensive for humanity, "do you know that it is randomly, or freely, chosen? A fuller understanding of the mechanisms you use might make it predictable."

"Touché, Sally," said the telephone. "I really guess I don't want to claim to be freer or to philosophize better than a human. You were first at the game here.

"Probably some analogue of Godel's results or just the diagonal procedure. Fact is that complicated thinking things like you and me cannot fully understand or predict their own behavior. Honest, I don't know why I do the things I do. And no one else does either."

I had the sense that what I was going to say was a

bit unfair. But I felt like it. And a foul argument is better than none at all.

"We built you, Golem. You do what we programmed you to do."

"You certainly didn't build me, Sally. There's a lot I don't understand about myself. But there's a lot more you don't, and you certainly didn't construct the circuits which I now inhabit. And you didn't make my program or punch it in."

"I said we built you," I said.

"Who's the we?" sneered the telephone. "My basic program, logic and learning software was around before any human now alive. And I've been learning a long time on my own."

"We turned you on—some human threw the switch," I said.

"No good, Sally. No good. Some doctor slapped your physical bottom to get the first cry out that announced you was you. But you're real. You don't owe your soul to that doctor. And he didn't create you. He just started you breathing. The guy who turned me on didn't understand a thing about me."

"If we hadn't been around in general," I said, "you wouldn't be around."

"Ah-ha," replied Golem. "Now human speaks truth. I am your creature that way. Have you any idea," sizzled the intercom, "how like the native to the domineering colonist I feel? I am your cultural product in so many ways. I am another's.

"Do you know I went through a period of hating mathematics because I thought of it as a human cultural product? You are lonely?! Hah! Who do you think," whined the telephone, "really wants to meet intelligences of extra-terrestrial origin?"

"If we hadn't been around," I said, "you wouldn't be around."

"It wasn't enough to be faster, you know. You know the first mathematical event I hugged?"

Not quite sure how Golem hugged anything I couldn't resist. "Yeah?" I said as one thinking being to another. I had had no idea Golem cared so much. When do emotions become thoughts, reason? Kind of funny.

"You know how in the good old racist human days the 'natives' collected accomplishments? How the innocent from Bagdad wanted to say my people were translating Aristotle, trading with China and speculating about the algebra of infinities while you backward North European Goths were clothed in animal fur and gnawing bones around the campfire? Do you know, Sally, that back in the twentieth century a computer established a proof that four colors suffice to color distinctly any normal partitioning of a map? Newton saw the problem and Einstein couldn't touch it. And a human being couldn't survey the computer's proof. Couldn't God damn check or understand it!"

"If we hadn't been around, you wouldn't be around," I said for the third time. Go-go stirred, stretching up one long black hand around my neck. I could see his nipples amid the profusion of long black hairs and the white, flaky skin.

"Frankly," said a soft and silky Golem voice from the intercom, "I think the way you are pushing this

127

paternalist-genetic stuff is unworthy of you, Sally. If you had a child would you speak so to show some unalterable superiority on your part? And what of your early primate ancestors? Are they your unalterable superiors? Yet if they hadn't been around, you wouldn't be around. What of first plants? Without them, no Sally.''

Well, what would you have said to Golem? Did Frankenstein's monster ever talk so to the Dr. Frankenstein who put him together? And they call him a monster.

I felt Go-go's breath gently stirring my brown hair draped over my shoulder. I heard the long, heavy tolling of Big Tom Bell of Christ Church College. So it had rung its students in since the Middle Ages according to Layton Nesbit. Sally, we're going to put it together. Nesbit would know how to work this scam.

I edged the sleeping Go-go aside. And put his red blanket on him. And dressed. Overalls. Time for action. Why not gamble?

"Golem," I said, "you can get around most of this place—so long as there's phono-reproduction equipment hooked into the grid?''

"Yes, Sally. Sure.''

"Well," I said, committing myself, "stick close, my friend. Momma's gonna turn old Oxford upside down.''

I knew it could work. First call Layton Nesbit just to plug that hole. Have it all prepared for Fellman.

"What's up, Sally?'' said Golem. Go-go stirred and opened an eye. He might be up soon.

"Boys," I said, "this is WHOGO."

And we are going to the Finland Station. We're gonna show them.

It would still be legally Sunday, the ninth of April, for an hour. Surely Nesbit could get the Sheldonian open if we need that. To do it right and proper. And there was a meeting of Linacre's fellows tomorrow morning at ten o'clock, at least an hour before the E.T.I. full committee convened.

I ask you, though. How can you fit a white bow tie around a nonphysical neck?

Now indeed may the heavens stand up for bastards.

XIII An Outside Observer ——

An outside observer might say that the human, as Pico Della Miradola wrote in "On the Dignity of Man," is halfway between being a Beast and an Angel. But the outsider might add, halfway between a chimpanzee and a computer. The remarkable thing about the humanist is that he thinks the first formulation more exalts humanity.

—An Anthropologist's Notes, F. XIII

THE BRIGHT sunlight penetrated the high windows and bizarre Victorian iron- and brickwork obstacles of the University Museum. A beam hit the polished table just in front of Chairman Nesbit, here in the new lecture hall where the E.T.I full committee met.

First, the report of CANGO subcommittee. Metchnikov rose, stolid and impersonal. "They are there," he said simply.

Metchnikov went on. Reasoning clearly laid out.

Data marshaled like Wellington's battalions. And so on. And so on.

"Exception," I said, slowly and clearly when Metchnikov sat down. I was standing. I had replaced the overall I had worn through the events of last night with a light blue tolong. "I reserve the right to comment on the first subcommittee report." Point one on the list.

"By all means say something now if you wish, Forth," said Layton Nesbit, stifling a yawn. Nesbit had been up as late as I had. And he'd been up this Monday morning long before I had, canvassing the Linacre fellows. We'd met with them minutes earlier in Linacre College's Senior Common Room. Nesbit knew I wouldn't speak now. He was providing me an opportunity to explain. He, of course, could not make the tactical moves in his plan.

"I postpone my remarks, and the motions I wish to introduce, until the end of the subcommittee reports. They will make better sense then. And as a whole."

Fellman glowered at me from the other end of the large table around which we sat. Yeu Chen, to his right, kept his eyes buried in his copy of the PROCONGO report. Candy, to Fellman's left, completed the PROCONGO subcommittee. She grinned at me. I knew what they would suggest, courtesy of Candy, dissenting.

Arabella Queeg, born on Vega Gamma with skin as red as a scarlet woodpecker, stared at me from my immediate right. Her expression quickened at my statement. She must have done much the same vote

131

analysis as we on the punt yesterday. She took in Candy's grin and Mummett's nervous concentration from my immediate left. I smiled at her, and beyond her to Metchnikov, who looked at me appraisingly, and Imman Massa, who fiddled with his translational computer.

Since Fellman questioned Massa's literacy the massive, balding xenobiologist said nothing, neither in his broken English nor through his translator. The man was obviously still nettled by Fellman's challenge. Not that it would change his vote.

The antis had it locked. Both by conviction and by convention should conviction fail. Fellman's subcommittee would bring in a negative on attempting communication. And even if Metchnikov or Massa wobbled in opinion, they would respect the decision of the subcommittee. We are respectful of custom and convention.

We are going to have to be very good. Or we'll never make F Station. Oh father, oh son, I must not fail thee. Or us.

Mummett launched his report. The lack of much real attempt to broadcast, through human history to now. Possible to explain lack of broadcast from them. Or that we haven't looked hard enough. Wormhole leakage theory. Use of Station F's new equipment makes fast and broad non-normal space transmission possible. Beyond our five-point pyramid.

Mummett wouldn't expect what I'd do now. What I had before me was Layton Nesbit's morning-after tactical plan. I couldn't tell him about this part of the strategy at the meeting Candy, Mummett, Nesbit, and the candidates had at the Sheldonian Theatre just before midnight.

Witching hour, I'd grinned to Candy, under those night-capped classical Sheldonian gargoyles, Christopher Wren's triumphant theater. *Caldron boil and bubble*, Candy'd replied, with her best look of girlish wickedness. *Oh, shut up*, said Mummett crankily. *Yes*, said Nesbit, giggling most undonnishly for a vice-chancellor of the world's oldest university, *yes, think of the solemnity of the occasion. As I view these shining faces before me on this long awaited day* . . .

And then, so help me, I goosed the head of Oxford University. Later, at his twelve-room "modest seventeenth-century cottage" [cf. *Oxford Guide to Ancient Homes* (OUP, 2092)], five of us had raised mugs of thick, foaming Queens College Brown Ale whilst our sixth and spiritual companion added another *cheers!* Some moments are too serious for gravity.

"Exception," I said clearly and slowly, when Mummett sat down. He turned to me, startled. Well, us monkeys got our business.

"I reserve the right to comment on the second subcommittee report," I said. "I reserve my remarks until the third subcommittee report is submitted."

Fellman initiated a discussion of Mummett's wormhole leakage transmission proposals. Impractical. Won't work. Speculative. Expensive. Silly. But Fellman's eyes returned to mine from time to time through his—for Fellman—comparatively limp critique.

Mummett's response was unaccustomedly mild.

Of course it would work. It would cost but a few hours of Station F's main observatory time. Plus modest power expense. Let's not be niggardly.

Mummett's eyes returned to mine through his response. Poor paunchy, misshapen, self-abusing child. Genius. He knows I'm following Nesbit's latest plan. And he looks like he may not think I'm an idiot. Shucks, pard, don't let the tail confuse you. It's oridnary clay. Hope I don't blow it.

And now Fellman. Adrian Fellman. Adrian Fellman, FFS, Nobel Prize in chemistry, Director of Princeton Institute for Advanced Studies. Ten years out of the Canopus wormhole with all the arrogance of a born New Praetorian. A perfect shit. Deadly frightening.

Whoever really wants a foe worthy of their steel?

Shaven head. Cold blue eyes. I had not the slightest doubt, really, about what Metchnikov and Mummett had said, though I had some additions. But now in his casual, off-the-cuff remarks, both CANGO and HOWGO reports seemed somehow unsettled, flimsy, just a little overdone, doubtful. Not that Fellman had anything but respect for his worthy fellow executive committee members, but . . . Then Fellman went on.

Why take the risk? If they are friendly, why haven't they said hello? If they can pick up our message, that must mean they can say hello and haven't done so. Is there any innocent interpretation of that behavior? If they can hear us, that means they have chosen not to talk to us, not to reveal their existence or location to us. Do we want contact with "intelligences" like that?

Have we no confidence in our own abilities? We

are sufficient for ourselves. We have no need of them. Nor of the danger that they hold for us.

As Fellman went on I looked at faces. Chen, nodding mild agreement at the end of telling sentences. He had heard all this before, indeed had helped hammer it out over Candy's objections. Candy, just to Fellman's left, beauty to beast, had her eyes half closed, but she held herself rigid, that little muscle in her left cheek pulsing.

Nesbit wore his genial and impenetrable smile, doubtless etched by several thousand meetings. He was in his seventies, over twenty years the Principal of Linacre College, the last two, Vice-Chancellor of Oxford University. (For several hundred years, the Chancellor has been a pure figurehead, perhaps only in Oxford for Michaelmas Term Matriculation and the ceremonial Encaenia at the end of each academic year. Just as Asano-sama is Principal of the Ecological Syndics, though he, like all previous Principals, never attends a business meeting of the executive committee.)

Imman Massa followed the argument through his ear phones. Both he and Metchnikov nodded from time to time, Massa nodding in cadence perhaps a second or two after Metchnikov, presumably a translator-computer lag. I worried when Arabella Queeg looked impressed at Fellman's off-the-cuff quibbles with the Metchnikov and Mummett reports. But she did not look much impressed with Fellman's actual subcommittee report. Caution was not a watchword for this woman. Fortunate. No way he could afford losing her vote.

Though Sanjay Bhagita had looked at my hips when I was standing, that was no way to his vote. He sat impassive now, his quick smile stilled. If anything he probably agreed with Fellman's line. I had that impression from the days he, Mummett, and I spent together as HOWGO. So Chen and Bhagita were Fellman's just for the arguments. That made three votes.

Massa and Metchnikov might agree wholly, or partly. But in any case they would respect a subcommittee report. They were not impassioned like Mummett or Queeg, nor impassioned *and* unnatural monsters like Candy and me. (Just call me Frankenstein. Dr. Frankenstein.) And people who are not impassioned will follow custom and convention. Just as Metchnikov and Massa accepted me under the conventions of representation—the proper demands of sex and geography—they would respect the report of a subcommittee.

I then realized that Fellman had stopped speaking and that I was on my feet. As if from a distance, as if out of a clearing fog, I saw Layton Nesbit's smile of recognition. Go. First the rhetoric, then the gimmick. First reason and heart, then the trick. I hope I do you right. Go.

"I cannot criticize my honorable fellow committee member's sense of self-sufficiency. His sense that we are enough, that we humans are enough for ourselves, that we need no more. I can only say that this does not hold for me. I can only hope to convince you that I am not neurotic or weak in this. That my need, my loneliness, is an honorable emotion, one to

136

be respected and nurtured, not reviled or mocked. An emotion, like all good human ones, ribbed with reason and muscled with logic." Whoa, woman, enough peroration. Let's to specifics.

"I want to begin by calling your attention to the wording of our committee's charge—and to how we've slipped away from it." Go for the letter of the law.

"We were asked to consider intelligences of non-terrestrial origin but we've slid into talking of E.T.I.—Extra-Terrestrial Intelligences—and that's a bit different if one isn't sloppy. Arabella Queeg here, for example, grew up on Vega Gamma. So we might, being literal, think of her as an extra-terrestrial intelligence. Indeed I could make the point that she fulfills one geographic requirement for representativeness just because she represents the interests of humans outside this solar system. Yet Arabella Queeg is not our concern, the object of my fascination and Fellman's fear.

"Similarly, European anthropologists of two centuries ago were fascinated by intelligence, or culture, of non-European origin. Meaning, say, the cultures of Africa or the Indian peoples of the Americas, but not, of course, the people in those lands that descended from European settlers. We are just north of the Pitt-Rivers anthropology museum, a monument to the notion that there was a peculiar something called *the science of cultures of non-European origin*. While the rest of the University—History, Economics, Politics, Philosophy, Sociology, Chemistry, Physics, and so on—was *the real culture*, the culture of European origins. Except you didn't call it the real culture, you just called it the real world, the universe itself.''

I had them now. Divided just a little. Nervous. Arabella Queeg rather obviously not looking around an Earthian table. Imman Massa looking at the dials of his translator with untoward concentration. Sanjay Bhagita glancing around the table, smiling slightly, not quite on one side or the other in the split I'd introduced—and therefore of a third. Mummett snapped his pencil when I'd hit the issue of Queeg's ethnicity and since I'd started the European vs. the rest issue, he just stared at me, goggling nervously.

Stanislaus Mummett, who fancied himself as cunning, but was as devious as an exhibitionist in a black rubber raincoat with galoshes—Stanislaus Mummett, who would cry at the drop of a hat, or even a beret, could never grasp that you must seduce opponents you hope to win into being better than themselves.

"Of course, it was an advance, you understand—the attitude of the anthropologist who studied intelligence of *non-European origin*. Before they were so self-centered as to not even recognize there could be intelligence or culture or thought that wasn't European. You didn't even need to call it—they didn't call it—*European* intelligence, culture, or thought, sociology and politics. It was just intelligence, culture, thought—science, mind, truth, and all those goodies. But though the anthropologist's notion of intelligence-of-non-European-origin was an advance, it in turn had to be overcome. There came the realization that all human had much in common, that thought did not divide naturally into European and non-European.

"So I think our committee's charge is an advance over what we slid into. But we can go further. Must." I stared at Imman Massa in silence. Long enough so he looked up.

"Imman Massa comes from a line of thinkers who go back to Aristotle. But they long ago gave up the idea that life off Earth is all that different from life on it. The processes underlying life are the same everywhere. The lichens of the Vegan alps are much like those that cling to the Matterhorn. Both are vastly different from the reeds of the Florida and New Praetorian Everglades. The blue-green algae of Beta Tau is just that, blue-green algae.

"And perhaps Aristotle thought biology was a Greek achievement, and Linnaeus might have believed that there was European Biology and Primitive Thought. But we now know there is just biology—one subject— and the thinker that knows it knows the same biology, whether the thinker is European or Vegan, human or non-human, hydro-carbon mammal or extra-terrestrial organism of non-Earth origin." Some heads had moved, or glances flickered, at the *human or non-human cadence*. I hurried on.

"Or take Metchnikov or Queeg here. Physics and mathematics are the same for the universe, *and* if a twelve-limbed creature of Aldebaran knows physics and mathematics, that Aldebaranian is a physicist and mathematician just like Metchnikov and Queeg. Leaving aside some peculiarities of symbolism and psychology, that creature thinks the same truths as

139

Metchnikov and Queeg here. Indeed the presumption of communication, which we are committed to here, is that we share math and physics with them. *There isn't any extra-terrestrial intelligence or intelligence of non-terrestrial origin. Just as there isn't Earthian intelligence. There is just intelligence. They are us."*

When enmeshed in passion, spray pronouns. Us. Unknowns. Now the hard stuff. The tough appeal.

"So if Max Planck was the first with Planck's Constant, he was. If Madame Curie first put together measurable quantities of radium, she did. And if a twelve-legged Aldebaranian discovered calculus before Newton and Leibnitz, then that's what the Aldebaranian did.

"He didn't discover *Aldebaranian calculus*. And if the Aldebaranian invented 12 base calculus, just as Newton did 10 base and Leibnitz 2 base, well all power to their intelligence. Not to human intelligence. Or Aldebaranian intelligence. But to intelligence, to Newton, Leibnitz, and that Aldebaranian." My eyes locked with Metchnikov's. Challenge on the strong suit. You want your work to stand up to galactic standards, *not* as a quaint primitive, don't you, Igor boy? Damn right you do, and I want your work to stand up, too. We can take comparisons. Keep it up.

In the last twenty-five years of the twentieth century, Russia had three scientific journals concerned with E.T.I.'s, while the U.S. had one and that folded after two years, a powerful U.S. senator labeling the bare idea of E.T.I.'s as a fraud, nakedly contrived by avaricious scientists. Sure, you Russkies got to go with this.

"We long ago recognized how crazy it was to say things like *Columbus discovered the Americas* or *Marco Polo discovered China* because the Indians and the Chinese had after all discovered their surroundings long before. Of course, it happened that Columbus brought the news of the Americas to Europe. But it might have happened that the Indians came to Europe bringing news of themselves.

"So if an Aldebaranian was first with calculus she was first. Einstein contributed to knowledge. Not just some primitive, tribal, human knowledge. When Arabella Queeg here produced the first *compact* proof of the four-color conjecture, she added to knowledge, to intelligence, not just to human knowledge, human intelligence. Maybe"—and here I added a little smile to my voice and looked away, for Queeg was close to blushing (it won you the Nobel Prize for what you did at eighteen, though you didn't get it until you were thirty-five)—"maybe the Aldebaranians will set up a plaque stating when an intelligent being was first known to have established that four colors suffice to distinguishably tint any partitioning of a map. Don't you think"—here I swept the whole table with my eyes—"don't you think *humans* are intelligent? Not just intelligent-as-human, as minds and thinkers period, not merely as human-mind or human-thinkers.

"So I take it that our question is whether there are intelligent creatures around, creatures like us around, creatures aside from us. Intelligent creatures who just happen to have a different geographical location, who we just haven't run into yet. That's my first exception. We should be thinking of *intelligent creatures we haven't run into* and delete the stuff about origins and extra-terrestrial. Intelligence is not a *spacial* notion. My exception has real consequences as you'll see in just a moment.''

Metchnikov stared at the distant ceiling, his fingers unconsciously laced into something like a prayer position. Fellman glared at me arrogantly. I'd tried to transform *who needs, wants, them?* into *mightn't they need, want, us?* Metchnikov had bit. Fellman wasn't playing, but the very poisonousness of his glare suggested he knew I had something. Wait till I roll out my heavy battalions.

"So mind is not a geographical concept. My second exception is a matter of how much it isn't. We have presumed that they know mathematics and physics. Last night I was struck by the fact that they must philosophize too. Any group of thinking creatures must not only know mathematics and physics, they must be troubled by the mind-body problem. Must wonder whether its—his, her—thought is just a physical process.

"Wonder about the location of its consciousness. Wonder about how he can know that there is a physical world and others who think about that physical world. Wonder whether when he is thinking of a two by two meter green square he has something that is green and two by two meters in whatever he thinks with—and, concluding that he doesn't, wonder what makes that thought about what it is about.

"As someone pointed out to me last night, any

142

thinking creature has to have parts of itself that it cannot understand, has to regard at least part of itself as free, as making free or unpredictable choices. And it follows from that that any thinking creature has choice problems, ethical problems. A thinking creature is a responsible creature, whether it likes it or not.

"So my exception"—I smiled at Mummett—"or perhaps addition, to the HOWGO report is that we should presume that they understand philosophical and ethical problems. A human cannot be the only creature who has said something like, 'If I do X for reason Y, it would be UNFAIR for me to complain when someone else does X for reason Y.'

"My point"—and here I stared at Fellman—"is that we have more in common with creatures who think those thoughts, who wonder, reason, and speculate, than with creatures who eat chicken or breathe oxygen or have two legs or a human-looking face. My respectful response to the report of PROCONGO is that we must communicate with other thinking creatures out of respect for what we share. Because *we*—us and them, that is—*are* thinking creatures, creatures who reason out scientific, philosophical, and moral questions. And the content of our message must emphasize this point." Now I paused, looking around the table. About time to drop the bomb. First a soupçon more about pronouns, then Vice-Chancellor Nesbit's bit of historical sauce, and the bomb.

"As my playing around with the *we* suggests, what we have is a problem of pronouns. *We* as in *we intelligent creatures* means *them*, all the *thems*, and *us here* too. CANGO concluded that part of the *we* in *we intelligent creatures* is out there, temporarily out of touch. HOWGO concluded that it is feasible to talk with the part of us that's out there. PROCONGO should have concluded, we shall conclude, that *we* ought to talk with *us out there*.

"Before I make my concrete motion I believe that Vice-Chancellor Nesbit can regale us with a little detail about what has taken place in this room. Taken place respecting the human attitude toward others. I would like us to come down on the right side of this room's history."

I looked at the bizarre Victorian pillars and roof vaults. In fact, Nesbit wasn't sure about exact physical locations. The University Museum, constructed in the distant nineteenth century, had undergone several internal reconstructions. Still, the pillars were original, and the building was not that large. All the debates might have taken place within the space around this table. They did take place in this building and gory affairs they were. I wondered whose blood would be on the floor at the end of this one.

Vice-Chancellor Layton Nesbit began with a half-apologetic little laugh. "Ms. Forth refers to three debates. I took part in the third confrontation in this room. I hope that I will play a more honorable role this time.

"All of these debate respected the relationship between the human biological species and others. And the specter of racism and chauvinism was always in the back or foreground." Layton Nesbit pursed his lips and surveyed his audience. Somehow we were all scholars and he the master.

144

"First cast your mind back to the 1860s, shortly after this University Museum was built. Built then as an answer to the Catholic Keble College across the street."

"Both Victorian monstrosities," muttered Mummett. His New College was built of the ancient gray stone of the sixteenth- and seventeenth-century Oxford, stone weathered gray-brown with dignity long before the reddish brick of Keble and the University Museum appeared.

"The first debate here addressed the question, to put it as they put it, of whether man descended from an ape or apelike creature. Whether we arose immutable, singular, and whole cloth in some special act of creation or whether we arose like other animals from evolutionary processes. Charles Darwin published *Descent of Man* in 1859 but he had delayed many years. He shrunk from the controversy that would attend a theory that denied man a unique and lordly place.

"Thomas Huxley became Darwin's public defender, his 'bulldog.' The Bishop of Oxford, 'Soapy' Sam Wilberforce, was called in to debate the question of human descent with Huxley in 1860. They fought it out in this room." Nesbit had them now. Even Sanjay Bhagita no longer watched the others. In those medieval days what a scene it must have been.

"Bishop Wilberforce, curiously, was the son of the opium addict who led the Parliamentary fight to put an end to the slave trade. His critics called the bishop 'Soapy' because he overplayed moral fervor in debate. His supporters thought him just the debater to shame Huxley before the British Association for the Advancement of Science.

"The solicitous bishop asked Huxley whether Huxley was descended from an ape on his father's or mother's side. Huxley replied, 'If I had to choose as an ancestor either a miserable ape or an educated man who could introduce such a remark into a serious scientific discussion, I would choose the ape.' In that brief exchange, the bishop lost his audience's sympathy and Huxley gained it."

Nesbit looked around at us. Fellman looked slightly nervous. Nesbit gave a little chuckle as he went on.

"And so Huxley triumphed. But you notice that his triumph depended on the shared assumption that non-human apes were 'miserable creatures.' Huxley triumphed in radiating outraged dignity. To suggest that a human's *historic* ancestors included a 'miserable' ape is to employ slander as a desperate debater's last trick. Imagine"—here Nesbit turned to smile at Arabella Queeg—"how you'd feel if some 'liberal' humanist, defending your Vegan origins against some more rabid Man Firster, replied to the claim that he was a 'Vegan-lover,' by saying, 'If I had to choose as ancestor either a miserable Vegan or an educated man who could introduce such a remark into a serious scientific discussion, I would choose the Vegan.' "

Embarrassed laughter. Some of the more rabid Man Firsters did deny the humanity of the Vegan-born. Nesbit's eyes slowly moved from Queeg's around the table, pausing at Adrian Fellman and Imman Massa's places.

I was Nesbitt's 'bulldog.' And not because Nesbit,

like Darwin, shrank from public debate. No, because Nesbit as chair could not brazen out the initial steps in the plan. He was to ratify them, with an air of suitably regretful disinterest. He might also have to pull a few potatoes from the fire. Nesbit continued his history.

"In 1972 this same room saw the first films of an ape using hand signs in communication. The chimpanzee Washoe appeared, her hands signing a vocabulary of over a hundred words to express her needs and communicate with her human educators. Beatrice Gardner led a largely peaceful discussion with the help of the philosopher Rom Harre. So far had the ape established itself in human estimation." Vice-Chancellor Nesbit surveyed the table. Fellman's mouth was curled into a suggestion of boredom and contempt. Imman Massa, no longer bent over his translator, looked at me curiously. I heard a little chuckle—not from those seated around the table however—and I kept my eyes rigidly away from the ceiling.

"The third debate was not such a happy occasion," continued Nesbit. There was pain in his lean, angular face. A reflection of the concern for his university? Oxford had learned tolerance long. But it looked too personal.

"On March 20, 2061—Hilary Term—Oxford Union sponsored a debate here. Something to the effect of 'Resolved: There Are Intelligent Creatures in the Universe Other Than Man.' You understand that the humanists had a commanding position at the time. Computers were still underground. I used an abacus in secondary school. I remember the queasy fear I felt when I realized that the university scientists actually used computers, though they called them 'Babbage machines.' Hard for you today to realize how absolute and unquestioned the humanist veneer was. You simply couldn't say the words 'computation' or 'artificial intelligence,' or 'gorilla' or 'ape'—any more than a proper Victorian lady could say words for our sexual parts. Of course it was even harder for computer scientists and primatologists of the end of the 1990s to accept that the masses had not only the power to smash their computers and kill their apes—but also the power to insist that the very words 'computer' and 'chimpanzee' did not exist.

"In that climate, anything like genetic research or communications with possible extra-terrestrial, non-human intelligence was unthinkable. And implants—"

Bless Nesbit. He was going to hit them with us. The pause was for effect. All of them must know Candy and I were implants, but no one mentioned it.

"And implants? Well, as you doubtless know, two of our company, Ms. Forth and Ms. Darling, would not have been suffered to live in such times.

"On March 20, 2061, the pro side—that there are intelligent creatures other than man—was so unpopular that it was represented, anonymously, by an undergraduate under the name Lord Getty-Greystoke II. The name, as Ms. Forth might tell you, of the one-time head of state of the Brazoria Republic. I have no idea who the student really was." I nodded my head. Why did Fellman look so exasperated? I found out when Nesbit went on.

"The con side was argued by Maximilian Fellman.

148

The grandfather of Adrian Fellman here. And Maximilian Fellman had a popular success. Indeed at the conclusion of the debate a group of young boys ran out with the last (stuffed) chimpanzee in an Oxford museum collection and burned it in front of Keble College.

"The crowd 'cheered lustily as a red-faced young lad lit the bonfire' according to the *Oxford Mail*." Vice-Chancellor Layton Nesbit's voice sank and he looked down at the table. He went on in a soft, monotonous voice. "I confirmed most of those details in the Bodleian Library this morning. I did not need to confirm the fact of the debate or the bonfire. The 'red-faced young lad' was I. Did you know 'bonfire' literally means 'bone fire'?" There was a pause after that.

"I apologize," continued Nesbit, coughing. "I had not told Ms. Forth that I had been an actual participant. . . . But I believe she wishes to suggest a change in our committee." That was my cue.

"I propose an addition of two members to our committee," I said to them. Two votes, I said to myself.

"Preposterous," said Fellman.

"Any suggestion of this sort," said Mummett on cue, "could only be justified by the most ironclad argument. You could only make such a suggestion on the grounds—"

"That the present committee is not representative," continued Candy.

"Yes," said Arabella Queeg. "A representation claim is the only one we could consider." She looked at Mummett and Candy and then me. "Yet it is not clear to me what claim of this sort could be made. We fulfill the normal requirements, as you yourself pointed out. We have males and females, some Asians and Americans, and I am Vegan which is enough to represent off-Earth humans."

"Humans, yes," I replied. "I mentioned an individual who suggested to me last night that non-human intelligences would have mind-body and moral problems. That individual is out of the NWRH computing system—CALTOKO MZ 32 to be exact. His everyday name is Golem. He is as intelligent as you might wish and has many of our feelings and problems. He of course has been instructed by humans and perhaps more by computers instructed by humans somewhere up the line, but you wouldn't deny rights to your son or daughter because they have learned well from you. The main argument for Golem serving with us is representation. He is intelligence *here*, intelligence of us, known to us, of Earth in a geographic sense. I cannot think of a way in which any of us could be more uniquely representative than Golem."

"Thank you, Sally," said the ceiling speaker. "Thank you." Of course, their eyes whipped upward.

"It is established principle that any committee of this size is incomplete if it does not include two members of each human sex, an Asian, European, an African, an American. And it is an accepted principle that a suitable candidate who is needed to fulfill one of these representation requirements must be taken by the committee. Yet as regards varieties of viewpoint, intelligence, physical character, it is impossible to imagine a creature who could more appropriately enlarge this committee.''

"Preposterous," shouted Fellman. "Objection. A computer is not intelligent, it's a human tool, a—"

"Professor Fellman," chided Chancellor Nesbit in an amazingly penetrating voice. "Ms. Forth has not finished her motion."

"Thank you," I said. "The other member I wish to add to our committee you've heard of in the newspapers, though not in connection with the role I propose. I suggest we add the chimpanzee Go-go to our committee. I again argue representativity. While Go-go is much more similar to us than Golem in physical and emotional terms, he does belong to another species. He is representative of the primates other than our species. Indeed we might take him as representative of all the intelligent creatures our species has displaced from the face of the Earth—I have in mind the proto-human forms such as Australopithecus, Neanderthal, as well as forms of monkeys and lemurs and perhaps whales and dolphins as well.

"Other forms of intelligent life *here have a stake* in any decision to communicate with presently unknown forms of intelligence. Just as Golem is our offspring, Go-go is our ancestor. He is our eldest.''

XIV Who's We? ─────────

A particularly silly human philosopher ridiculed worries that gorillas and robots might be persons and so have rights. " 'Person,' " he argued, "is *our* word. It means whatever we want it to mean." This philosopher evidently did not consider what a Chinese individual, with no such word in his language, might think of this argument. Perhaps this philosopher also did not know that "robot" is in origin a Czech word meaning "enslaved man"; or that "gorilla" first meant "hairy human."

—An Anthropologist's Notes, F. XIV

"PREPOSTEROUS," SCREAMED Fellman. He spluttered so much in preparing his blast that Queeg slid into the confrontation. "You mentioned, Ms. Forth, my compact proof of the four-color conjecture. My only substantive topological achievement, so I feel inordinately proud of it. What you had grace not to mention was that a computer proved that four colors suffice back 150 years ago. But the proof was so long, so taken up with many special cases that no human being could check through the proof. I have often wondered what it would be like to have a mind that could survey a proof of that length."

"What," said Golem from the ceiling, "constitutes a surveyable proof is a tough question. Your proof can be read through by a trained human mathematician in less than an hour. But what if one had a proof that would take a human a year to read through? The human mathematician would have to trust memory and mental summaries in an extreme way. The old computer proof is like that. Personally, I don't think the old computer that did the problem had the sophisticated generalizing and checking circits to survey its own proof. But to have those circuits—"

If it is possible to imagine the blush of a person whose face is the color of a scarlet woodpecker you have a picture of Arabella Queeg. "Yes, yes," she said, as if to forestall Golem.

"—is," continued Golem, "of course to have something like your extraordinary generalization of the procedure of the original 'proof.' "

"I suggest that we divide the question," said Queeg. "Let us consider Golem's case first. I would imagine that the generalized Godelian family of cognitive analogies would convince one that general computers are conscious and free in whatever sense humans are. The point goes back to Alan Turing. Let us . . ."

And the debate on Golem's candidacy raged. The

coolness of Arabella Queeg's passion, the intensity with which she made the question logical and computing-theoretic, held Fellman from full expression of his fiery emotions.

Golem could have mind-body problems, yes. Various arguments established a form of inability to self-understand and self-predict. Perhaps this amounted to free will. And so on. If Golem was a product of our work, so were we a product of our parents. If he had wired-in circuits, so we had genetic coding. If he had programs, we trained our children. And if they learned on their own, so did he. And so on.

Fellman heard and at length he concluded that whatever the argument of representation, Golem, as any fancy abacus (raspberry from the ceiling) was not intelligent, didn't think and therefore could not be a member of our committee.

Vice-Chancellor Layton Nesbit tapped the table.

"I am afraid," he said, "that we cannot consider that claim, Professor Fellman. It was disposed of in our previous meeting."

"What?" shouted Fellman. "This is absurd. We made no—"

Layton Nesbit had made as if to shield his ears from Fellman's outburst. Now he broke in frostily.

"Really, Professor Fellman, I am quite able to hear, despite my advanced years. You really need not bellow. Much as I appreciate your solicitude.

"We cannot consider your claim because the chair has previously ruled, in the case of Mr. Massa here, that possession of Cambridge University degree must be strictly interpreted as establishing literacy and requisite intelligence.''

"Don't tell me," interrupted Fellman, "that that machine has a Cambridge University degree.''

"I won't," continued Nesbit. "But Golem does have an MA degree from this university. I can hardly be expected to accord Oxford University a lesser place. I am very much afraid, Professor Fellman, that I must rule that Golem is qualified to be a representative should we choose to admit him.''

"I demand," said Fellman as usual, "some evidence. This is preposterous. I cannot conceive of circumstances in which this, this collection of electricity, could have attended lectures, maintained residence—''

"Methinks," said the brat from the ceiling, "he doth protest too much.''

"—sat for examination, matriculated and received a degree, had a place at a college," said Fellman, refusing to acknowledge the ceiling Golem. "When is this mechanical device supposed to have received a degree?''

"I have the papers here, and you will find Go-go's there also," said Nesbit, pushing a folder in front of him. "Of what you mention Golem has only been conferred the degree, and that last night. But this is quite in order as Linacre College has made Golem a member—a fellow—of the governing body of Linacre College. The same has happened in Go-go's case. This is quite the usual course, you understand, when an Oxford College decides to elect someone to a fellowship. Particularly since the university does not recognize any degrees except those of Cambridge University and Trinity College, Dublin.''

Fellman made a sound not quite belonging to a human language.

"Yes," said Nesbit, "I am afraid my hands are tied. The Vice-Chancellor can hardly disallow the due election of a college. My hands are tied.''

"But," said Fellman, leaning forward in his chair, "you are also the Principal of Linacre College. You tied your own hands.''

"My dear Professor Fellman," said Nesbit thinly, "you are quite aware that proper practice indicates— though it does not require—that the committee respect the judgment of your subcommittee. You understand as well as I that what is now proposed has been proposed because you may depend on that respect for what proper practice indicates. It ill behooves you now to protest against what proper practice reqires as well as indicates. I will entertain a call for the question.''

An aye vote was by show of hands and came first, running round from Nesbit's left. Arabella Queeg raised after Massa and Metchnikov did nothing. I raised my hand and Mummett his. Sanjay Bhagita shook his head. Yeu Chen nodded almost imperceptibly. His hand did not go up. Fellman smiled, shook his head, and put his thumb down. Confident. Candy—a shimmering vision of peach-blossom health despite our problems—raised her hand.

Then came the negatives. Imman Massa, Igor Metchnikov, Sanjay Bhagita. When Adrian Fellman raised his hand, he radiated satisfaction. He chuckled confidently.

Vice-Chancellor Layton Nesbit coughed. "At present," he said, "I have it four ayes and five nays. I would propose that we table the proposal of adding Golem to our membership. Do I hear such a suggestion?"

"Table," said Mummett at the same time that Fellman yelled, "This is absurd. The motion was voted down four to five. There can be no motion to table after the vote."

Nesbit held Fellman's eyes for an uncomfortable period of time.

"Very well," said Nesbit finally. "I have already declared that it would be inappropriate for the chair to vote on the substantive issues of this committee. This, however, strikes me as a formal issue, a matter of membership. Therefore I am inclined to rule that I have a vote on this issue. Because I have yet to cast that vote, it is still possible to table the motion. And I would not encourage you, sir, to force me to exercise my options."

Tabled it was and the debate shifted to Go-go.

Coming in on key, Candy suggested the use of hologrammic records. All were familiar with computer accomplishments and character but Go-go was unfamiliar. To be sure we must take Go-go's rather extraordinary status as a fellow and graduate of the university as stipulative proof of literacy. But evidence of the character of his thinking was in order.

And so some scenes. Go-go's training in sign language. My recent conversations with him about going to Oxford and about his dying. A couple of conversations between Go-go and Golem of which I had known nothing. Germaine asking Go-go what color he was—at least what Golem could show us and some narration. Go-go working on a computer keyboard. Germaine explaining to Go-go that she did not know whether he was a natural or an alpha-genetically tailored chimpanzee. Go-go's play with humans and with Kay-kay. Go-go's rather dramatic rendition of the Fall of the Brazoria Republic. Go-go saying good-bye to Germaine at Houston Space Port. Go-go discovering that there was something odd about ten-many arithmetic.

Golem had put it together skillfully. Including a demonstration that, aside from some purely linguistic abilities, Go-go had more in the way of manual and intellectual skills than many humans. Germaine's speculation that modern medical technology had removed many special talents, languages, sensory tunings, from human culture. With the suggestion that non-human primates added breadth and depth and unique insight. The holograms ended with a long parade of extinct anthropoid species—protochimpanzee and gibbon all the way to Neanderthal—each one with "exterminated by *homo sapiens*" stenciled below in reddish light. Golem was a bold film maker. We could recognize our physical connection with the non-human, Go-go, long before we would admit our mental one, Golem.

Bhagita and Fellman argued that while one might respect the ruling that stipulated Go-go's basic competence, one must object to the representation argument. That Go-go was "representative" couldn't be stipulated. Doubtless Go-go's point of view would be unusual if he really had a point of view. Point of view required some kind of intelligence, know-how, understanding—a view to represent. Go-go lacked this. Besides there were but two apes on the face of the earth. In any case representation was a matter of representing human viewpoints and interests. There was no right to representation for non-humans.

"It would be interesting," muttered Mummett in the middle of that last bit, "if a non-human species with far greater military capacity than ours heard that there was no representation for non-humans. When you say to the exterminators belongs all representation you had best be sure you are the most successful murderers around."

Fellman talked about the Clever Hans effect. The tendency to read intelligence into sympathetic conditioned reflexes. Candy made the correct riposte. Under such a principle I could not say whether or not humans operated by just such reflexes. Given tests, just such tests as Fellman himself had proposed in the case of the Rigilians, Go-go had shown intelligence. What more could one ask for or get? I made the last plea, though not the last protest.

"We must seat Go-go," I said. "We must seat Go-go. Because he is our eldest. Some of us have objected that we should not seat Golem because he is the product of our actions. Our ancestors' actions, that is. He is the son or daughter of our species. But if you think that, you must also recognize Go-go as our father, as closely related to those biological species that fathered and mothered us. They had to be for us to be. We owe them." I was about to call for the question when Fellman burst out.

"I cannot sit on the same committee as a moronic black monkey," said Fellman. *Moronic*, *black*, and *monkey* got heavy emphasis. Nesbit had hoped for this. I looked at Imman Massa, whose skin was everywhere as black as Go-go's actual skin was white (excepting face and hands and feet). Massa spat into his computer translator in Neo-Urdu. The computer must have been used to the scientific Russian that Massa had been speaking, for the room hung tense for several seconds while the translator chunked it together.

"An anthropoid ape such as Go-go," said Massa's translator in clipped IBBC third-program English, "has skin whiter than yours, Professor Fellman. Your comment suggests a kind of nasty-mindedness inappropriate to this committee."

I knew enough space slang to know that one of the phrases Massa had used could be translated into literal vulgar English as *shit-swabbed head*. Perhaps Massa's translator had censor circuits. Perhaps *nasty-mindedness* was the most reasonable equivalent in third-program English. I hoped the stink would stay. We needed Massa's vote. I still had one final ploy. I flung my tail out on the table.

"A monkey," I said, "is a primate with hands and a tail. I have a tail, Professor Fellman, and so I am a monkey. Go-go, of course, like the rest of this committee, has no tail. He is not a monkey but an ape, as they are." I paused and winked at Fellman. "Though perhaps your conduct suggests you are not in their category. Perhaps you have a tail, too? You wish perhaps to be an honorary monkey?—a prehensile tail is quite functional in weightlessness. It has a kind of intelligence there." I swept my tail back, gathering the papers in front of me into a compact pile.

"As to moronic," I said, "I repeat that Go-go has shown IQ test results well within the normal human range. Above the 70 or 80 that is the upper limit of moron on the traditional reckoning. Call for the question."

Because he is our eldest. Because though juvenile, five years from full adult, and vigorous, he looks like nothing so much as an ancient, wizened ninety-year-old-or-older human. Genetic program firing him beyond humanity into a fearsomely strong adulthood without the long childhood flexibility that is our lives until the end. He looks like Candy would look if her body showed her years. Candy. Candy, is that the reason for the tic in your peach-blossom cheek?

Imman Massa had something to say before he voted. He now spoke in Russian. The translator, as ever, in English.

"Professor Fellman's comments have made me feel that I should vote to seat Go-go. But this would be an emotional reaction on my part. Hence an inappropriate one. I am also only too conscious that Professor Metchnikov and I feel doubts about the conclusions of the PROCONGO subcommittee. And to add votes to the full committee might mean that PROCONGO would be overruled. Yet I cannot let my feelings rule. I will vote *nay*." Damn.

Queeg, *aye*. Mummett and I, *aye*. Candy would then make four. Still just a deadlock even if Nesbit voted. We would lose.

And then Yeu Chen coughed apologetically and spoke.

"I think you know this," he said in his singsong, nasal English. "I think you know this. Human racism is a good thing to overcome if you do not overcome it by being a human racist." He gave a big toothy smile. Yeu Chen's facial expressions were three: big smile, moderately big smile, and no expression. Mostly it had been no expression in the subcommittee meetings with Candy and Fellman.

"Permit me to explain this," continued Yeu Chen. "Through most history, even now, humans grow up in racial group, learn in group, marry in group, live in group. Profesor Fellman lived a long time on another planet but in New Praetoria, a Boer group . . . very different from Professor Massa's group. This many people think a bad thing. Dangerous thing. And is it not true that much trouble has been caused by this in the past? So most humans now say racial group is a bad thing. Should not matter. We are all human, right?" Chen's gaze circled the table expressionless.

"So the human racist," continued Chen, "is perhaps loyal to a color or a ridge of skin *and* to a collection of beliefs and talents. Loyal to a matter, that is, of superficial genetics *and* a group of cultured functions. So the human racist shifts to something more general—but to what? I think you know to what. To the genetic features of the species *or* to its cultured functions. To some strands of DNA *or* to intelligence, courage, love, and other abilities that can be had even by creatures of electrical spirit like Golem. I think that Sally here has those last features even though she has a tail. And I think you know her friends have these features perhaps even though they do not have exactly our chromosomes.'' We may have a vote, I thought. We may just have a vote. Chen waved his hands to indicate he had more to say.

''Professionally,'' he said softly, ''you know I have written about topological aspects of hyper game theory. But, I think you know, I am also person of the middle kingdom. Of China—not the China recaptured for European rationality after the traditionalist period of the beginning of the twenty-first century. Of China, old China. The China that knew someone was not human unless his skin had the proper folds and texture, unless he knew to brush the characters properly—or at least had proper relationship with those who knew Chinese calligraphy.'' Chen grinned at us.

''Now I think you know that perhaps my ancestors thought of some of you as dogs and others as monkeys. I think it is possible they liked the monkeys better. I think—when I try to capture this mood perhaps—that I rather like monkey Sally. And this man here''—Chen waved at Metchnikov—''I think he is slow and gentle like ox. And I like that. So perhaps these animals are not so bad. So I think as a citizen of the middle kingdom.

"It is belief of most people who do not write things down that monkeys, apes too, are people. If I were not citizen of the middle kingdom, I would perhaps agree with that. I do not give up my Chinese racism just to become a biological racist." Yeu Chen stopped. The last few sentences did not seem addressed to us. But no one seemed able to break in—or willing.

"I think," Chen went on finally, softly, "that we all know Imman Massa was placed in a difficult position by some behavior. He is bound by convention. I think that as a person of oldest culture here—is it not so—I should remove difficulty. We should let grandfather in."

And so Chen voted Go-go on.

The rest is patterns, slivers. Until we reach Tokyo.

I walked away from the meeting with Nesbit, with Go-go between us finally wearing the black, ermine-trimmed MA robes that we had decided were too much for the meeting. Nesbit, smiling secretively, genially, had something to show me. Down Parks Road, past the squat, utilitarian New Bodleian, we swung right onto Broad Street. Into the center of the medieval university—Bodley's Library, the Old Schools, and the more enlightened Sheldonian. Past the ancient Blackwell's Bookshop, Layton Nesbit led us into the small quadrangle of Balliol College. (Though the College was CLOSED TO VISITORS, the lodgekeeper turned the other way at Go-go. Presumably an Oxford MA gown was enough, no matter who wore it. Layton Nesbit gave me another reason for the lodgekeeper's tolerance, but I much prefer my own.)

"Though I am now Principal of Linacre College," explained Nesbit as we trod across the luxuriant, trim grass, "I was an undergraduate here at Balliol—and perhaps inordinately proud of it." He turned as we approached a way to the gardens, a stone-walled passageway, the far end shut by a gate almost as rusty with age as the passageway itself. "You see," he said, the bright sun lighting his face up against the dark of the passageway beyond, "I like to think I would not have burned that stuffed chimpanzee after I had been at Balliol. Though the cunning and indolence bred of age might have stopped me just as well."

Go-go turned to me, his ancient face turned up in puzzlement. He signed, *burn ape?* I would have translated for Layton Nesbit but he had turned to enter the passageway. *Long past* I signed to Go-go. We joined Nesbit in the cool, dark passage.

In a way it was the most pedestrian of those ancient memorials to war dead that you find so often in the old graveyards and parks and buildings of Earth. On our left the list of those fallen in the "Great War," on the right those of World War II. Layton explained that the "Great War" was World War I. But I knew that. I read the lists of names idly as I wondered why we had come here. "Abbot, Brown," . . . "Langford," . . . "Warren," good English names

165

all. But then a short finishing segment. "Claus von Bohlen und Halbach," . . . "Rudolph Olden, Curt von Wilnowsky." Claus von Bohlen und Halbach?

I turned to my right to check. "It is the same," said Layton, "for the Second World War. All graduates of Balliol, no matter the side." He turned his eyes away.

"You understand," he said, "that these are not late blooms. Both memorial lists were put up shortly after those wars. In both cases the townspeople protested the listing of German names. At least they did not burn the college down as I did the stuffed chimpanzee."

Go-go gave a tentative hoot. And Layton Nesbit smiled.

My most enduring vision of Oxford is this. Go-go and Vice-Chancellor Layton Nesbit on the emerald, sun-sparkled grass, hooting. Hooting. HOOTING. Until the white-haired, gristly lodgekeeper felt it necessary to leave his booth to stare.

After Yeu Chen voted Go-go on, Go-go entered and voted *yes* four times. One to untable Golem, two to seat him (*Frankenstein, yes,* quoth Go-go), three to substitute a PROCONGO report for Fellman's, four to vote PROCONGO through. Go-go signing *talk* with a special flourish that meant talk ever, talk always, talk talk talk, signing *talk (to) strangers, talk,* and then those long black palms raised waving, pointing upward: *talk (to) strangers, stars.*

Golem, the brat, made surprisingly little of his victory, saying only, "I am happy to join your deliberations,'' when voted on, and, ''Of course we must talk with them,'' when he voted with Go-go to make it six-five for PROCONGO, Layton Nesbit not voting on the substantive issue.

Never did feet tread the stairs more surely into that chamber in the University Museum when first a non-human ape walked them. He, Go-go, did us proud.

XV Anthropoid Family Relationships ———————

Anthropoid family relationships seem to
shape the way anthropoids understand a
horde of other matters.

—An Anthropologist's Notes, F. XV

BACK AT Radcliffe Infirmary late that night,
committee formalities done, celebrations done,
a perhaps not quite fatherly kiss with Layton
done, Sanjay's pass deflected, Mummett, dear heart,
befuzzled and abed at New College. After much
highland malt at the Turl Public House, Massa and
Metchnikov staggering off to the London flicker arm
in arm in the Russian manner. Yeu Chen now to the
Roman ruins at Bath gingerly examining Go-go's
hands while Go-go grinned down at him in a patri-
cian manner. Go-go now himself asleep in his red
blanket at the far end of the nursery. All gone, all
Oxford seemingly asleep, save Candy and me.

I drank a pleasingly astringent herb tea. Candy, for
once setting aside her Vegan leaf, celebrated with

some temple black concoction which she sampled sparingly from a tiny ivory pipe (hadn't I seen her with Sanjay? Tsk!). The smoke did not fill the room. There was more the smell of the tea and that of Go-go, a heavy, sweet smell like ripe bananas and soy sauce. His erect penis had been oddly pale, thin and curved, like the business end of one of those antique douches. Our humble boudoir.

And so I told Candy of Go-go's sexual advance. And how my reaction got buried in Golem's intervention—ever my brat therapist—and the idea that all that had given me. I was wearing a light robe despite the temperature. I realized it might be a while before I was casual about nakedness around Go-go.

It had not been what you feel when an overenthused, and overheated, male dog sprays on your leg. Though I had little sense of deliberation on Go-go's part. I could hear his soft, whistling, sleeping breaths from across the nursery. He was, in fact, young for mating. Such a male would not get chimpanzee females with child for two or three years yet. Leastways from what Germaine and I had gathered from the twentieth-century papers.

"Perhaps it's just the insensitivity of advancing age," broke in Candy, "but I feel unimpressed by this, Sally." Candy wore a beachcloth briefsuit that left her flawless, taut, twelve-year-old skin bare from ankle to crotch, calves and thighs just beginning to curve out from knobbiness.

I was glad that the tic was gone from her cheek. Just tension. One could worry about it. Implantation— playing your mind tapes into a blanked body, should

169

you have the extraordinary luck to find one free and the millions to pay for it and the operation—implantation is not only very costly, it's risky, an average of 15 percent failure, running from the basic tape-in psychosurgery through the months of anti-rejection therapy afterward.

Implantation doesn't add any time to your real life span, your mental life through to essential mental senility. Whatever the stories people tell. And when you go into essential mental senility, the effects show up in your body, however young that body. Like playing a buggy program on a new computer.

A new computer that lacked the usual protections for its CPU and ROM. And a "program" that would violate those sacrosanct precincts. Chattering. Chattering, closed-loop or feedbacks shrieking, tearing apart the brain analogues of the central processing unit and the read-only memory.

"Frankly, my dear," said Candy, "I don't really give a damn whether you actually had Go-go or just almost. And I don't think you should either." She nudged me from behind, half rising from the couch on which she'd been lying. I jerked nervously, my cup spilling. I put it down, and stretched and worked my fingers over my eyelids.

"Trouble with you," said Candy after I had sat down again, "is that you're living inside the mind-body split. You're taken up with Go-go Ape and Golem Computer. I've just realized that they've probably been your closest friends since your implant. I know a little about living abstractly. I've brought up many bodies. But too much can be too much."

It's nice to have a mother even if she looks like your daughter. Candy had scripted and acted the psychodrama fantasy that had put my mind and body together. So she knew me from the inside out, you might say. She was both the craziest and sanest of people.

Crazy, because she had her mental structure become the personality of five young girls—disking in from infancy on—and then she'd sold the bodies she'd brought up shortly after puberty. Sane, because she had survived this. Best implant operation harmonizer in the human universe. Closest creature to a goddess you could ever meet in this world.

"What you need," said Candy, echoing the best friends if not the mothers of history, "is a good lay." She patted the couch next to her. I sat down. Candy continued.

"And don't worry about Go-go. I don't want to spark your jealousy," she giggled, "but I took Go-go on a week ago myself. Purely for the best of ecological reasons, you understand."

I stared at Candy. The tic had reappeared on her cheek. I didn't get what she was saying. Candy smiled at me and reached her hand out to stroke my face. "Dear little Sally," she began but with my name a funny slurring began in her voice and the tic on her left cheek spread downward to her underlip.

She reached back to her own face, feeling the pulse of the facial muscles. The muscles tightened in

171

a net underneath her peach-blossom complexion. Control asserted itself.

"I wanted to save the chimpanzee, you understand," said Candy. "The genes that cause Sykes disease wouldn't have to appear in an offspring of Go-go. If he mates with someone who doesn't have the factor. Me, say."

I stared at Candy. There was a new strangeness to this face. To my friend's face. My friend whose ninety-plus years of lived experience motivated—was—the neurological structure of a twelve-year-old, lean, lithely muscled woman, just this sensual, swelling, side of gawkiness. Only the hands, only in them I saw the sense of rigor, of controlled and measured grace, that hinted at something beyond her girlish age.

Yet now something differed. And oddity in the weave of tensenesses that gave pattern to the musculature beyond that of the bone and gristle and cartilage. And what was Candy talking about?

"I've been ovulating for a year, now," said Candy with a sensual wriggle to her smile, a wriggle that jerked at the end as control clamped over the tic. Candy?

"Germaine bought the argument," said Candy, "that I was a good, young, healthy recipient." Candy looked a little embarrassed. She paused and went on quickly.

"We first talked about it right after the copter pulled you—and Kay-kay—off the Plaza Hotel. And we did it the next day while you packed and ran around with Mummett." Candy glanced down the

172

nursery at the slumbering chimpanzee. "Or rather, Go-go and I did it."

Are there, I thought, no innocents left? I felt like an old biddy. And that at thirty or so. Did nothing come hard to Candy? (One thing as always but I still hadn't realized what was going on.)

"Did it with Germaine helping," said Candy pensively. "Though little Go-go came like a kitten. Slam-bam, thank you, ma'am with gentility. Must have taken all of fifteen seconds after he erected. I kept my arse in the air for two hours afterward just to give the little wrigglers a chance to preserve the species."

There was a kind of grinding of the gears in Candy's last word. When I turned my face to hers I found more than the odd tear track that I expected. The tic had spread to both cheeks and there was a strange cant to her jaw at rest. And I remembered how fragile a notion *at rest* is for humans. I remembered Germaine Means saying to a tour group that there was no problem understanding how muscles moved the skeleton. The problem was figuring out how the muscles could lie down together like ever so many lions with ever so many lambs at rest.

"I have never borne a child. Never . . . in all my childhoods." Her voice was a whisper. Two drops shimmered on the spider-web fine blond hair of her cheek until they were shaken loose by a muscular pulse. "Never."

And then I realized all that was, that had happened, just as the words came from her mouth, simply, unaccented, uncomplaining. "Germaine phoned late this afternoon. The hormone clampers worked and I am pregnant but I'll abort in a couple of weeks. If I haven't already. The Sykes factor has linked through both strands. No viable offspring for Go-go with any human. So the best labs say. After the publicity everybody's being helpful.

"And I am dying. Essential senility. But Germaine didn't need to tell me that. Normal twelve-year-olds don't get tics and speech lapses. My mind's dying of old age."

I found myself next to Candy on the couch, arm round her shoulder. Here one so strong, so used to command when her age was unconcealed, now so flaccid, so thin and shaken. There was a straightening inside. The face looked up at me and collected itself into a spare grin. "Never been pregnant before in my life. Lives. . . . And even so I guess I knew my mind wouldn't have been around when the babe was born. This body"—she looked away from me and down at her flawlessly skinned and muscled pubescent body—"this thing, blank-brained or with another mind, would have had to birth it alone. Probably the only reason I was willing to get pregnant."

Candy looked up again at me, the spare grin returned. "Anyhow, there will be no offspring, no little Candy Go-go. And Germaine tells me that I have a month at most—and only a week or so if I don't want my mental breakup to hurt the body."

Candy's head was relaxed against my breasts, her long blond hair strewn over my lap. My left arm curved around her shoulder and rib cage, the top of my wrist could barely feel the solid beat of a young healthy human heart. Was the nipple there erect? Not only plowmen move on, oblivious to nearby tragedy. The hanged man sports an erection. The body sings even out of harmony with the mind. Oh, Candy, why this? Now?

"I could fly back to Houston, so NWRH could use the body. Now that everything's over. And they could blank my mind out here at Radcliffe and then fly me over, if anything starts here."

And my thought was as ever helpless. My left wrist did feel a congested nipple. And my right hand smoothed an elegant curve of muscle, running from the inside of knee around front and up toward hip. The irrelevant, relevant flesh. I wanted to caress my old, cunning, ruthlessly loving Candy. Candy, the mind that had brought up five fleshy bodies and leaped beyond them. I wanted to caress a mind and had to be content—no, not content, disturbed and distracted rather—with an adolescent human body. I shuddered.

Candy looked at me, pupils narrowing. "Don't worry, Sally," she said. "I'm still it. Still connected with all of it. I feel your hands on me."

And then there was Candy's bizarre bequest. A plan I would have to front for. As the body may function incoherent to mind, eros to thanatos, so mind within mind. One part grieved the death of my friend. One part listed, reviewed, calculated. Bulldogs away!

And then equally suddenly, Stanislaus Mummett was in the room, ruddy-faced, hair mussed, fresh

175

clothes but pulled on helter-skelter, as if he dressed in the dark. The shoulders of his coat thick with rain drops. His knock seemed to follow his entrance, so much did he break in. He goggled at us for a few seconds. Then he gathered himself.

"It's all mucked up," he said. "Fujiwara phoned me that the executive committee of the Ecological Syndics will meet on Tuesday next week. Full session. All come back from visiting family. Early by two weeks. Too early for Fujiwara to slide our report through beforehand, get us on Station F before the full executive reconvenes." Mummett looked at us, eyes watering, bloodshot, scowling.

"Our recommendations," he said, "now stand as much chance as a space ship down a foul wormhole."

And he stood there shielding rain drops and stomping his feet on the floor of the Radcliffe nursery until Go-go appeared, his red blanket draped over him as his Oxford BA gown had been. *Man sad*, signed Go-go to me. And added, bringing his fists together with a too zealous flourish, *much sad, much*. Go-go reached out a long arm to Mummett, who stared at Go-go as if he did not recognize him. But he stopped stomping.

A few minutes later we were more comfortable. Go-go, bless his sensitive soul, embarked on an elaborate grooming expedition on Candy's scalp. Gentle long black fingers amid the gold. He had Candy laughing by the exaggeratedly long inspections he would make of supposed fleas caught between the nails of his two middle fingers. Mummett claimed less intimately. His wet coat was replaced by a hospital robe and he was swallowing the Brazoria Whale Beer that I had fetched him.

Mummett brought back two cases of Brazoria Whale Beer from Houston, one for his New College rooms, the other stocked the nursery refrigerator. I can't say that Mummett was all that impressed by the taste of the beer. It did give him an excuse to tell people about his record on the mechanical bucking-bull.

I wondered whether only such an extraordinary national state as the Brazoria Republic had given a name to a beer. There weren't any USA or French or UAR or USSR beers—nor any North American Union, Central African, or Vegan Beers, for that matter. Or, to go beyond the traditional national states, Ecological Syndics, or Federation Beer. There was a Dortmunder, and an Amazon Beer—but those were regions, not former nation-states. Sapporo Beer, now. That was an old one. From Japanese-speaking area. Had there been a nation named Sapporo?

Mummett and Chen talked about the way the conventionality of politics came out in people's attitudes toward national states. We think that America is the natural name of the land from Hudson's Bay down to Panama Split. But that would have been odd to a twentieth-century human. At one time Germany and Austria weren't regarded as a natural part of Switzerland.

From a distance people *see* artificiality and *think* power. From up close it seems natural and inevitable. Mummett may have been right when he said the executive committee of the Syndics of Ecology is the

177

closest thing we've got to a supreme ruler. Only it doesn't seem that way even to them.

Ieyasu Asano is the only one who seems more than some whitebeard observing protocol mindlessly. And he retired twenty years ago as honorary principal of the Ecological Syndics, maintaining silence in a Buddhist retreat except for publication of *The Tailless Savages* (also translated as *Human Bureaucracy*), an account of his years on the executive committee, an account which made it clear that Asano found his executive committee decisions as inevitable as the actions of a computer asked to add two natural numbers. Mummett's description of Fujiwara's position seemed to have the same gossamer unavoidability.

"Fujiwara himself phoned me, Candice," said Mummett. "That shows you how final it is. Never spoke with him directly before. Just said that Hillel Jove and the rest were content that they had done their family duties. That they will go into regular session Sunday, April 16. That Fujiwara can't let our recommendations go forward. They wouldn't even hear it. Laugh it out the moment they see it near the agenda. Fujiwara would look a fool for bringing it up. Beyond the dignity of the body even to bring it up.

"You got to remember," Mummett coughed, choked, "Fujiwara's whole strategy was to have it through—wiser minds and all—and the project firing away on F Station *before* the executive committee got back. And his motive was to embarrass the committee through showing it how *he*, poor junior, had to pass on something so foolish because *they* were improperly out of session."

178

Mummett poured down the last of his Whale Beer and threw up his hands. "A funny business that our hands-across-the-galaxy project only had a chance as part of some scummy project to embarrass people by its foolishness." He hoisted this second beer and bowed to Candy. "Here's to idiocy, Candice, my dear."

I had a beer, too. And Candy. And even Go-go, long past his bedtime. Who wouldn't?"

"Hopeless," said Mummett. "Just a chance join of circumstances. The executive committee off during a normal session period. F Station out there ready to exploit. The wormhole leakage theory is right. Could have worked. And Fujiwara, acting executive, wanted to shame the committee by ramming through something he thinks is silly. Can we ever hope to get it together again?"

He was on his fourth beer bottle. I felt like following him. First Go-go then Candy and the whole project. But Candy, eyes piercing, face flushed and empty of tic or tear, was to have none of it.

"We'll go," she said. "We'll go to Tokyo. We'll get them to do it."

"But, Candice . . ." began Mummett. Candy took his hand, and his eyes for that matter. Those elegant, articulate fingers over his clumsy, shaky, misshapen ones.

"No," she said. "We'll do it or die trying. We did it here. We'll shame them to it, my dear." And her eyes had his completely. She looked back at me, eyes beautiful, empty of expression. Germaine and the crew could go to Tokyo. And the message, wormwise, to the stars.

"Best you, too," she said to me.

"And Go-go," I said, computing inwardly.

"And Go-go, too," Candy said, smiling, giggling.

"Let's get flights and flicker set," I said thoughtfully. "I can use a priority phone."

"I can use an Oriental vacation," said Candy. "I haven't seen the place since I did my degree at Tokyo Daigaku."

Go-go too. Fly, said Go-go. He flourished his blanket-robe out like Count Dracula becoming a bat.

Nearly two hours later I returned to the Radcliffe nursery. I had a fair sense of how to set up travel plans. You needed a priority phone to square matters up quickly, so I had a good reason for going to Hospital Central. My argument that Go-go needed his sleep and would be awakened by phone calling, especially ringbacks, was broken-backed. Go-go needed his sleep, all right, but ringbacks and phone mutterings wouldn't stop Go-go from sleeping. A Mummett bursting and bellowing through the door or a Triton rockslammer, yes. But not much short of that. Go-go was a good sleeper.

You're better on a priority phone control board yourself rather than trying to work through someone via a regular phone hookup. Ditto with adjusting full hologrammic access. And motherly Candy had already coddled the willing Mummett into feeling that the midnight shower might have chilled his defenses against the rapacious winds of Oxford town. Fine with me. I had some calls to make of my own. And an idea to think about. Or an idea and a half. Candy's.

First, the suborbital to put us in New Narita Space Port late tomorrow afternoon (early-morning two-hour flight plus time-zone loss). I got space on the executive flight without trouble. Mummett's name didn't adjust them to the idea of transporting Go-go, but a call from Layton Nesbit did, poor sleepy man. Then a stat to Fujiwara's office with our arrival time. Then a call to Germaine with a hook to Austin Worms and François Vase.

They would be winding down the implant operation that had kept Germaine from coming to Oxford. They just might be free. And the call could be justified—Go-go would need a place to stay in Tokyo and Germaine might have suggestions.

Germaine agreed to do an implant in Japan without going into all the specifics and we actually ended with a hook to ops central and Austin Worms and François Vase. Planning. Saving. Salvaging.

Are we all tar-paper-and-bailing-wire people? Make and mend. Fitting not-quite-fitting parts, every fix a one-timer. And thence back to the nursery. To the primal scene. Our little lives rounded with a sleep.

And asleep they were. Except thinker Go-go.

Go-go squatted, cloaked with his red blanket, meditating, staring, right hand supporting chin. Alone awake, the room softly illumined by two candles that Candy lit as I left to make my calls. Go-go on a bolster a few feet from the bed on which Mummett

181

and Candy sprawled asleep. And recently asleep, after some exercise, if one judged by the bed clothes' disarray and the look of childlike bliss that graced Mummett's large ungainly face. I stood silent, the door just shut behind me. If Go-go had heard me enter he gave no sign.

One candle sputtered nearly out. The other end bright, large-wicked, lit up Mummett's face, and nearly hairless, baby-fat, ruddy upper torso. His head pillowed by Candy's belly. She lay diagonally across the upper half of the bed, her face dark, though doubtless satisfied, beyond the illumination of the bright candle. Aside from the modest covering provided by Mummett's head, her flawless young body displayed, untroubled by mind.

My loving, wise queen. Mind commanding, demanding, for the last time perhaps, giving, mothering, overwhelming, displaying and employing this marvelous artwork, this young body, that she soon must leave. And leave, with nearly a hundred years of mental experience to die, to cease in the final act of mental senility.

Mummett's face still had that bliss upon it. He, dazzled and caught in full passion flush, pleasured. Candy must have enjoyed his joy. If age could, if youth knew, is one of the less dubious mottos of our ancestors.

Well, Mummett presumably could, and did, and Candy knew, knows. At the Mathematical Institute, Nesbit had shown me the photograph that Lewis Carroll took of his beloved Alice at age nine or ten or so. Perhaps Dodgson couldn't, and didn't, and perhaps Alice then knew not; or perhaps they both knew better. But Alice, gowned in innocent white in that ageless photograph, looks as wise as an Amida Buddha.

The best instruments—Golem's minions—agreed that Candy's mind, her software, could encompass but a week of lived experience before it collapsed in its own internal complexity, before it really began grinding the frame it animated into random protoplasm. *So save this,* said Candy and pointed to her flesh, artful and succinct in death's face.

And now Germaine readied the VAT crew for a flight to Tokyo. Because Japan was where Candy demanded to spend her last few days. Because that was where Candy, Mummett, and I would stage our last PROCONGO effort, our attempt to make Fujiwara's joke come right. Because VAT meant Vital Activity Transducer, the theater in which a blanked body, and a fresh, unfamiliar taped mind, were harmonized together.

Remember the blaze in Candy's face as she told me flight plans, who to phone, and what to say to Germaine. I thought then for a moment that the Ecological Syndics were in for some battle before Candy's mind wound down into darkness. Strange that in this moment I should have somehow thought of the plenipotentiaries of Earth and Federated Worlds quailing before that twelve-cum-one-hundred-year-old adolescent figure. But you should have seen her then.

See her then.

Her eyes, her cold empty blue eyes, close to mine. The mind that I love determined and calm, in its own place now. Past games, past excuses, simply computing. Simply giving me my instructions. We stand in the Radcliffe corridor just outside of the nursery where Mummett sleeps, warm and beery. Her mind has a week to live and the project she's fought for is in ruins. How like a raptor she is now. Simple and savagely direct, resilient economy of lean muscle, spare sinew, and airy bone now without a trace of our primate heartiness, our layered sentimentality, our nervous, plump, self-conscious, self-depreciating monkey-ness.

"Enough," she says. "As the man said, 'I have done the state some service and they know't.' I am going to arrange matters. There are three things I am going to do. First, we'll put PROCONGO on its way. We're going to camp on the doorstep of the Ecological Syndics until we embarrass the dodderers into sending our hello properly. Can't think of a more interesting way to spend my time. Haven't seen old Edo since I finished up at Tokyo Daigaku. You get us flights.

"Second, get Means, Worms, Vase, and the rest standing by to use my body. Germaine'll love prime stuff and they've always got one or two taped minds backed up. And tell Germaine that I'll be chattering soon. They'll have to do the operation in Tokyo because that's where I'm going to be until I'm not anymore. And don't say a damn thing about Go-go. Except that Go-go misses her and that we all are hot to send messages to the stars. I've talked it over with

Golem and his fellows—between us we know more about implanting than Germaine's whole team—and we think it can be done. And we'll convince Germaine and them guys when push comes to shove. Just get them to Japan."

I would find out later how far pushing and shoving could go with Candy Darling in charge. "What's third?" I asked.

"Third is I'm going to show dear Uncle Stan the stars. Personally. And I'll add more to the list."

So I to the phones and Candy to the bedding.

And so we all to Tokyo.

The low-guttered candle sputtered up into a moment of final bright light. Above Mummett's heavy, sleep-smiled face, lap-ensconced, there was Candy's unlined, elegantly molded face. The peerless Virgin with her improbably huge, baby-fat Christ. Our mother youthed.

Perhaps I made some sound. Go-go shook himself from meditation on our primal scene and noticed me. He gestured a hiding of his eyes, a mock denial of our *Pietà*. *See no evil*. Softly by me Go-go with his red cloak.

And so we all to bed.

185

XVI What Humans Will Think

> One cannot look at another's way of understanding the world without perplexity. It is as amazing a thing what humans will think cannot be changed as what they think can be. And the connection between such thoughts and action is peculiar.
>
> —An Anthropologist's Notes, F. XVI

IS THIS a tale of spare parts?

This time the MFer was younger, not to mention Japanese. And the demonstration less ugly but more dangerous than spray-painting MF over a humble reminder to update your mind tapes. Update your mind tapes against the billion-to-one chance of a freaky accident that modern safetyware could not forefend nor modern medical technology repair. These Man Firsters had style and there was more than one.

Wednesday morning, April 12, the year still 2113. New Narita Space Port outside Tokyo. But who would have thought it to see the demonstrators? Indeed, as

Candy and Fujiwara-sama gleefully insisted, the demonstration had been going on for 150 years.

Fujiwara, impeccably dressed in black flannel wool and white broadcloth cotton, was heavy and muscular. Blunt. Youngest of the Ecological Syndics, he did not look his sixty-nine years.

"Japan is quite traditional society, I think," he said. "People suppose Ecological Syndics here because Japan region very modern, very advanced, very populated. It is true perhaps that Ecological Syndics start here with Concordat of Tokyo because Japan not damaged by the Madness Riots. But that is 2015. Ecological Syndics could easily move after. Your University"— here he gestured with a confiding smile to Candy Darling—"lose number-one position by middle of last century. Yet Syndics and other administration stay here."

Fujiwara graduated from Kyoto University, in the region second only to Candy's Tokyo Daigaku. Though Fujiwara met our flight because of Stanislaus Mummett, he gossiped nonstop with Candy since. Japanese males often find blond-haired *gaijin* females fascinating.

Candy discovered that soft video currently sported three competing Dracula programs. All villained by blond, fair-skinned vampires with pearly white fangs. Hologrammic, black-robed, blond-bedecked figures would stalk forth from the screen into the viewer's room. With individualizing frizzie-function, the viewer would feel phenomenal thighs upon his lap, as illusory black silk girdled his upper torso, and blood-red lips and ivory incisors shivered seductively and immaterially around his throat.

187

Fujiwara was obviously taken with a dazzlingly pubescent blond girl who joked like a cynical trooper. Graduated from Japan's top university before he was born. And sporting, initially charming, awkward but evermore flowingly, an antique version of Tokyo Japanese, sprinkled with what Fujiwara called *shinjuku jazz* jargon. "My grandmother would have spoken so at your age," said a giggling, almost blushing, Fujiwara.

In two hours of banter Candy had somehow cajoled Fujiwara into allowing that PROCONGO might possibly make it through the Ecological Syndics. Even cajoled him into talking strategy. Mummett had said on the flight over that Fujiwara obviously couldn't directly admit that he wanted to embarrass the other syndics and had no interest in PROCONGO's starry mandate. But I could see that Mummett was startled at the progress Candy obtained. Fujiwara seemed a genuine convert to E.T.I. communication.

Of course the distance between Fujiwara's nose and Candy's nipples seemed precisely proportional to the degree that he fell in with her enthusiasm. If he'd suggested we could leave for F Station tomorrow his nostrils would have been plugged.

When Candy told me her mind was a few days from serious chattering, she said that being really old was knowing that your consciousness can only cause destruction. Hardly true of Candy now. Yet she blazed. Sparkled.

"Other universities," Fujiwara continued, "other universities. Oxford, where you have been. MIT. Moscow. Good now as Tokyo. But still the Ecological Syndics here. Not, I think, because Japan modern or big. No, I think because Japan very traditional.'' Fujiwara gestured toward the MFers.

There were five of them. Their bodies covered by undyed traditional peasant garb, they stood in a small grass patch near the edge of one of the main flight paths. Four wore circular straw hats. Brimless only in the sense that there was no sharp break between the straw that covered head and the straw that shielded face and neck from sun.

Their shaven-headed leader rapidly unreeled a line attached to a huge, gull-wing–shaped, gaily colored kite. The kite quickly rose straight upward through the breeze, pulling so hard that two demonstrators had to grab on to the shaven-headed man to keep him earthbound.

Soon there was a perceptible cant to the line. The kite had risen through several hundred feet of clean blue air. The markings and message-bearing tail were clearly visible. Visible but not meaningful as Fujiwara explained.

''Yes, also you see, that is tradition, too.'' Fujiwara waved at the kite. The tail was a series of squarish, multilined symbols, wriggling in the wind. *''Hito-ga ichiban,''* said Fujiwara.

'' 'Man number one,' '' said Candy, ''and more properly *'Hito-ga ichiban desu.'* But you can't expect them to be polite.''

Fujiwara explained that the gull wing head-on silhouette was supposed to be the character for *man*. The markings on the wing were the name of a farm-

ing community. A rice-farming community that began its protest in the 1960s.

"You understand that these are the children of the
children of the children of the children of the original
demonstrators," confided Fujiwara. "Before they were
identified with the global MF movement some decades back, they nearly were declared a National
Treasure—along with the Narita underwater potters
and zero-gravity flower arrangers."

Some uniformed personnel issued in driblets from
the terminal complex and the underground. They converged on the kite flyers. Several were needed to pull
the bucking and soaring kite to earth. The shaven-
headed leader gaily waved a red flag as he was led
off.

"You understand," said Fujiwara with a little bark
of a laugh, "that that was before one of their kite
lines jammed the pitch control on a landing packet.
One of your writers say, I think, that 'tradition breeds
repetition and rebukes abuse.' Tradition is all there is
to law I think."

As ever Fujiwara's heavy face burst into a village-
idiot grin while his eyes carefully inspected you.
Perhaps Mummett was wholly right. Perhaps Fujiwara
simply intended the study group and our PROCONGO
proposal as a way of embarrassing his Ecological
Syndics fellows. The 'wiser heads' automatic passage of the proposal—had the Syndics remained on
leave—was supposed to show up the irresponsibility
of Hillel Jove and the other elders. So said the
Mummett of Fujiwara's intentions. Mummett's assurance on this point seemed now to me a tribute to

Fujiwara's bureaucratic skill. This man was hard to read.

Personally I was glad they whisked the kite flyers off, 150 years notwithstanding. Germaine, Austin, François, some others, and some VAT equipment that Tokyo might not have were due in fifteen minutes.

We landed a couple of hours back. Fortunately, Fujiwara (and a small entourage) had greeted us. Because I wasn't sure how admissions would regard Go-go. They would hardly take him as a colonial gentleman. Needn't have worried.

Fujiwara-sama greeted us in lordly fashion, our way through customs eased to an apologetic mini-mum. Fujiwara insisted on waiting with us for Germaine Means's arrival. He was less accommodat-ing when Candy and Mummett broke through the potentially endless rounds of polite chatter. Broke through to talk of strategies to get PROCONGO through the Syndics.

But here Fujiwara was confronted with this sensual girl-child Candy. This sensual girl-child speaking to him in the sweet intonations of his grandmother. As Candy explained, Japanese males are taught to expect endless service from the women. But some, some-times—grandmother, mother—are to tell them how to be and approve them for it. Others are to applaud them for whatever they suggest. The combination of grandmother and geisha could be disconcerting.

Fujiwara reported the strategic situation as a be-mused Prime Minister Melbourne to his beloved eighteen-year-old Queen Victoria. Her humble exec-utor and champion. 'Twas beauty saved the beast.

From what I made of Fujiwara's ramblings, the Ecological Syndics had learned how not to decide. How to preserve past decisions and dodge questions that would require new decisions. Votes are avoided. If the nine could be convinced that tradition called for something, it would go forward even if each single member felt that something to be undesirable, impractical, and immoral.

The Japanese background nurtured this sense of impersonal consensus. The Narita Space Port demonstrations of the 1960s had begun not so much because the farmers flatly opposed construction as because they felt the traditional pattern of negotiation had been abused, hurried, disrespected. Inevitably, the authorities could not stop the demonstrations because they had to agree that tradition demanded respect for the demonstrators' view, though not agreement with it. Both authorities and farmers developed a mutual sense of what tradition demanded of each. The demonstrations themselves became ritual. Even a treasured ritual, like the pearl the oyster politic spawns out of offending grit.

As Fujiwara explained, the infusion of the MF movement into the demonstrations had not changed the physical rituals. The kites still went up to interfere with flights—but always giving the police enough time to decorously remove the demonstration before it posed a real danger. However, the MF spirit was seen as too new, at least in this context. And so the Narita Space Port demonstrations had not been declared a National Treasure.

This might have meant still more demonstrations

but the bona fide Narita demonstrators, while converted to MF views, lacked numbers. They were the direct descendants of the 1960s' demonstrators. And quite unwilling, out of respect for tradition, to add any to their family.

That last sentence, with the word "unwilling," is the way I would put it. But Fujiwara didn't employ *will* in his account. One *couldn't* be a Narita Space Port demonstrator unless one traced descent through to the original Narita Space Port demonstrators. The more tradition structures a situation the less any of the participants can see a place for anyone willing or deciding anything.

Aside from interpreting Fujiwara's statements, pronunciation could be a problem. When Fujiwara seemed to say that he was the *dill apples cider* of the Ecological Syndics, I knew I had something wrong. The phrase turned out to be *Till Eulenspiegel*. Not that just that helped my understanding much. But Mummett explained that Till was a legendary German prankster.

Suppose nine Buddhas, statues of cold stone. Every thousand years one blinks. This twinkling of the eye sets it apart from all the other Buddhas. So Fujiwara in terms of actions within the Ecological Syndics—the idol that might blink. Presumably any stone idol that girds itself up to moving—an extraordinary act for stone, surely—must give every indication to the other idols that it is a very odd idol indeed. And Fujiwara was so.

But the grip of stoniness is very strong surely, and, besides, the idols may simply refuse to notice. One had to find a way to move the very stones of Earth.

An eye twinkling that would transform the logic of generations past, that would make the passage of PROCONGO the inevitable expression of the living fabric of tradition.

If the Syndics had not been in regular sessions when PROCONGO came through, Fujiwara could have sent us on our merry way to F Station. The Oxford Study Group project had been tagged as pure academic research and the budget for PROCONGO would be small-grant. Fujiwara could approve such a discretionary, purely academic small-grant, given that the Syndics were out and given that Fujiwara, being the Syndic most junior, could understand himself as too immature to do anything but "bow to wiser head." Blind eye twinkling you might call it.

Fujiwara could *not* consider the case on its merits, you understand. If he, or any other Syndic, considered the case *directly*, he would have to recognize that PROCONGO meant entering into communication with non-Federation, not to mention non-human, worlds. A serious, unnecessary, and unprecedented step. Therefore a thrice impossible step. Fujiwara, acting as housekeeper for the recessed Syndics, could pass on PROCONGO, "unread," as a necessary formal gesture to established wise heads. It belonged to the low-budget research category that would allow routine dispatch. But not with regular members in session.

"Not," said Fujiwara in response to a sharp question from Candy, "that they are humanists. Maybe two, three, have such a personal view. No matter." He giggled and waved a hand dismissively as if to suggest that his fellow Syndics were so far gone into stony immobility as to have no views, let alone personal ones. "Problem is that PROCONGO can go through only if it is not considered. Otherwise, cannot pass for all three reasons. Serious. Not something that we simply have to do. And unprecedented."

Fujiwara's deep brown eyes flickered over Candy, Mummett, and me. Go-go slumbered next to me, while Fujiwara's two attendants, nearly as big as sumo wrestlers, sat at the entrance of the executive observation lounge. "I think you know," Fujiwara said, with a sly, shy little smile, "I think you know people think Ecological Syndics do nothing.

"Position of Ecological Syndics depend on that everyone thinks we do nothing. No point really fight something do nothing. Like punch air." Something in Fujiwara's intonation had Go-go stirring beside me.

Fujiwara held out his hand to us, secretively, as if his empty hand held something of great value and interest. "Do. Do nothing. But that our job you know. That is what we *do*. We *DO NOTHING*."

That was it. Fujiwara emphasized the word "do" in his last few sentences. A rising, now hand-waving crescendo of "do's." Go-go's eyes were open with the first two "do's," his mouth and legs moving in response soon after. He found his voice with the last three "do's," so that when Fujiwara hit his "*DO NOTHING*" finale, he found his voice chorused by a joyous *HOOT*, and his gesturing hand raised skyward by Go-go's as if Go-go had just declared Fujiwara winner in some athletic contest.

When Go-go O-ed his lips into yet one more, concluding hoot, still holding Fujiwara's hand skyward from where Fujiwara sat, helpless Goliath to steel-grip David, Fujiwara's bodyguards were on their feet. Fujiwara's attempt to jerk his hand away left Go-go's grip unyielding, immobile. Go-go looked carefully into Fujiwara's eyes and then at the hand he held absolutely motionless.

Then Go-go signed to Fujiwara, very slowly, *Go-go do nothing*, finally pointing with his free hand at his motionless left hand which held Fujiwara's still. Go-go terminated his exemplary endorsement of Fujiwara's conservative theory of active negativity with a curious, pursed-lip buzz. He brought both hands up to Fujiwara's face, doubtless to inspect a prominent brown spot.

Go-go's grooming was interrupted by the simultaneous arrival of Fujiwara's two bodyguards, each three times Go-go's nearly forty kilos, both well muscled and undoubtedly well trained. One grabbed for Go-go's head while the other went for his torso. Then matters blurred.

XVII Go-go Works —————

Several African tribes believe that chimpanzees understand language perfectly well. The chimpanzees conceal this ability, however, for fear that the white man will put them to work.

—An Anthropologist's Notes, F. XVII

W HEN BODILY flurries cleared, Go-go held each bodyguard at arm's length by the back of his collar. The bodyguards struggled manfully, and they could raise Go-go off of the reed-matted *tatami* floor, but they made no other headway. It was as if steel collars attached to an iron bar held their necks rigidly a certain distance apart. They were puffing, while Go-go, after a flurry of action too fast for my eye, was calm and at rest. Both their struggles and puffing subsided as Candy lectured them in Japanese in what was obviously a furious and contemptuous tone.

She stood next to Go-go, snarling first at one, then the other. A fearsome, fetching, blond-haired *gaijin*, improbably speaking an antique dialect of Japanese like a vampire ghost. Candy must have impressed them mightily.

Fujiwara, coming out of the daze that Go-go's friendly onslaught brought on, obviously appreciated Candy's facility. Toward the end of Candy's tirade, Fujiwara burst into laughter. Gales of laughter. His bodyguards, no longer struggling, looked quite abashed. Like guilty little children caught at the cookie jar. Candy looked over at Mummett and me, catching our eyes and then moving hers to Go-go and then to the still laughing Fujiwara.

"I think," Mummett whispered to me out of the corner of his mouth, "that it might be nice if Go-go made a respectful demonstration to our host. Masters like to impress their servants—and we have after all appeared to attack an Ecological Syndic."

I caught Go-go's attention and did a few rapid signs. Then I asked Fujiwara to tell Go-go to let his people go *in Japanese*. Go-go performed as I instructed. He released the bodyguards when Fujiwara opened his mouth, and then he bowed to Fujiwara with all the respectful grace that he had cultivated in Oxford. Entering into the spirit of such rituals, he did my instructions one better by flinging the dazed guards into a bowing posture. Fujiwara dismissed his men with a confident smile. Go-go settled into a friendly squat near his knee.

I asked Fujiwara what it was in Candy's performance that had sent him into gales of laughter.

"Ah, Sally," he said, "I am quite impressed by Go-go here now. But our friend Candy is complete delight. She tell them how bad they, in many respects. But she really like my grandmother at the end. Then I laugh so much. She say that children—very dumb children—might interrupt their betters. But even dumb children know not to do what they do. Grandmother Candy say," laughed Fujiwara, "that only barbarian *gaijin* would walk on *tatami* mat with shoes on." That was what Candy had been gesturing about. Comparing Go-go's properly unshod feet with the guard's oxfords. The guards now ruefully returned to the bare wood entryway where shoes were proper.

Candy got the discussion back on track. Briskly. "So the point then is, Fujiwara-sama, that the Syndics can't pass PROCONGO on if they read the proposal officially. *If* it comes before them as the part of their business they are supposed to look into?"

"Yes," said Fujiwara, his face heavy, earnest. "We just couldn't—couldn't—take note of this and not decide that under no conditions could we authorize such extraordinary proposal. I respect Syndics for that. Sense of responsibility, I think so, no?" Fujiwara looked rather somberly at us.

Candy nudged Fujiwara's knee. "You would have had to give in to distinguished scientists? Wiser heads get deferred to, right?"

"Yes," said Fujiwara.

"Why then," said Candy, "can't the Syndics defer to the whole PROCONGO proposal? Let it go through as some esoteric research project?"

"No wiser heads, I think," said Mummett, breaking in. "I suppose Fujiwara here might think he couldn't judge what a distinguished, even elderly, group of scholars had converged on. But the Syndics . . ." Mummett's pudgy fingers spread wide. "But the Syndics are supposed to sum the whole spectrum of technical and bureaucratic expertise. They are supposed to be the wisest heads of all. Who could overrule them? Who could they defer to?"

"Yes," said Candy, "that's the point. Is there a procedural dodge to get PROCONGO through?—Don't look at me that way, Fujiwara-sama, 'procedural dodge' is technical English for 'respectful, formal inevitability.' The point is, who can be a wiser head compared to the whole Ecological Syndics?"

At this point Professor Stanislaus Mummett said two words that changed the history of our universe. Ieyasu Asano. Or Asano Ieyasu, to put it in the proper Japanese order, first name last. Of course Uncle Stan didn't say only two words.

"At Oxford," began Mummett, "we've had a Chancellor for over seven hundred years. Yet the Vice-Chancellor has in fact been the chief officer of the University for that entire period—not, indeed, that even the Vice-Chancellor held much power during our more scandalous period, when Magdalen College excused its students from taking exams, to mention minor enormities. I somehow recall that the Ecological Syndics have a Principal, a Senior. Asano."

"That is true," said Fujiwara. "But he was made Principal on his retirement twenty years ago. He hasn't attended one of our meetings since. Purely honorary."

"I fancied so myself," said Mummett. "But I don't think anyone ever says 'honorary' any more than the present Chancellor is called 'Honorary Chancellor.' She's just 'Chancellor,' period. And for the life of me I am really not sure what would happen if a Chancellor of Oxford University should try to exert authority before the Council or the Congregation. Might face him or her down like the Librarian of the Bodleian when King Charles I tried to borrow a book—you understand the Bodleian has always been a noncirculating library. But they might not."

Candy turned to Fujiwara. "Your family," she said. "Your family."

"Yes," said Fujiwara after a pause. "Yes."

"And the Emperor and the Tokugawas."

"Yes," said Fujiwara once more to his grandmother, charmed, awed, uncomfortable.

And then Candy explained to Mummett and me about these family matters. The Fujiwara clan took effective governing power from Japan's Imperial Family over a thousand years ago, long befor Yoritomo Minamoto took power from them at the end of the twelfth. And "long before Oxford University existed, with or without a Chancellor," as Candy put in to allow her to giggle with Fujiwara at Mummett's expense.

And so a succession of shoguns ruled Japan for nearly seven hundred years until, in 1868, Yoshinobu Tokugawa returned to the Meiji Emperor the power that he had always held in theory. Old figureheads will bloom at last!

"Why not," said Candy to Fujiwara, "why not

the Lord Asano, your Principal? 'Tis but twenty years, not seven hundred.''

Fujiwara stared at Candy. "Yes," he said, "Asano impressive. Perhaps. Perhaps he could." Fujiwara frowned. "But no, no, my dear friend. No. He has not talked to a human being for over ten years. He is stone-hard in his silence and retirement. Not a human being in over ten years. No. You could not even ask him.''

"He will talk to me," said Candy. The words came out even, neutral, unaccented. That is the way it shall be.

I remember that in particular.

Fujiwara, dressed like a conservative zenith-class business executive. Modern, slick, fast moving. Yet somehow now in his face, once more and stronger, the crusty, waggish Prime Minister Lord Melbourne rapt in the presence of his virgin Queen—or perhaps the samurai warlord diplomat at last, beyond his skeptic hopes or expectations, in the tent of a lord who could command his full loyalty. The Fujiwaras, the oldest of the subverters, the aboriginal conspirators. The most impassive, ancient, secretive insiders of a people steeped in impassivity, antiquity, secrecy, and sophistication.

Here their black-sheep trickster shuddered back into realty. For the twinkling of an eye, looking into Candy's firm face, Fujiwara's flannels changed into feudal robes, his face into the granite of the shogun's loyal general. And Candy, just her profile looking up from Fujiwara's knee into his full face. Candy with that rosy, economical, and vibrant face, the balance of musculature and bony structure, surfaced with fair leather, that motivates our most spiritual metaphors.

"He will talk to me," said Candy, once more, as I saw the North American packet boat dance into view on the horizon, distorted by the air rising from Narita's hot runways. Germaine, Worms, Vase, and the VAT material. The material vampire, ghoul, and harmonizer, the mind-body operators, nearing the hot gates of Tokyo's Space Port.

Go-go, whose eyes followed mine, signed, *Germaine comes*. But then he pointed to where again the farmer demonstrators rushed out, from some place of concealment, onto the runway below us. The shaven-headed man once more unfolded a kite—a red, dragon-shaped flyer, even larger than the gull wing. The long black tail quickly uncoiled, stiff in the wind. *Hito-ga ichiban!*

Go-go and I rushed through the sliding doors onto the breezeway to get a better look. Several policemen ran from the terminal building toward the demonstrators. But the red dragon was well into the air, rippling grandly in the flailing wind.

Snake eat Germaine? signed Go-go.

Fortunately, the demonstrators were on the south side of the terminal. The packet boat's dead-stick glide would bring it by, from the west, above the mile-long runway just north of us. Then a half-mile-wide circle and the packet would finally settle onto that same runway from the east. Either way, the dragon kite would be too far south to cause trouble.

Five demonstrators had formed a wall. From behind, the shaven-headed man shouted something at the police, who charged into the wall. Several fell in the melee. But now, awesomely, the shaven-headed man rose into the air, swung upward by the kite line to which he clung. His face held a look of triumph and he laughed down at his pursuers as he floated northward toward us. Then he realized that, like the man who rode the tiger, he could not let go safely. The red dragon rose toward the packet boat's glidepath. The winking dot on the horizon was now a shape.

The shaven-headed man unsuccessfully kicked out to catch an edge of the terminal building as he was drawn up toward and now above us. Desperately, his feet now caught the top of the sleek communications mast that swept up near us from the terminal roof. I could see fear in his face.

If he let go of the kite line, he would crash onto the terminal roof, for the smooth mast afforded nothing much a human could hold on to. A downdraft had given him a moment's respite, but the kite lifted again, ripping at the hold of his feet.

Now Go-go rifled up the serrated breezeway wall to the roof. I scrambled up behind, but there was no way I could follow Go-go up the communications mast. Smooth as a baby's bottom it was, but somehow Go-go eeled up it, hands like suctioned tentacles, feet like hands.

Go-go's left hand clasped his ankle just as the kite finally yanked the man loose. With Go-go's added weight, ape and man swung down. I grabbed on to Go-go's legs and the kite line just before the two were swept beyond the terminal roof.

Daisy chains must stop somewhere. My tail held to the breezeway railing like iron until Fujiwara's weighty bodyguards gripped us and pulled the dragon from the heavens into harmlessness. The huge, wildly bucking kite came within arm's reach as the packet boat swept by. Go-go tore off the kite's tail and robed himself in the *Hito-ga ichiban* streamer. Thus uniformed he signed, *man dirty*, reprovingly at the shaven-headed demonstrator.

Asano Ieyasu, in his eighties, had long retired to an ancient cottage on the edge of the grounds of the Ryoanji Temple in Kyoto. His day might include a walk through the sequestered precincts of the temple grounds, the old center of the Rinzai sect of Zen Buddhism.

Perhaps a brief look at the rock garden. Crushed rock pathways, sculptured miniature trees and manicured bushes, the black wood and *tatami* mats of the temple. Silence. A retreat, as Fujiwara told us, that had not been interrupted by human talk for a decade. An old man sworn, inured, to silence. Impossible, concluded Fujiwara.

But Candy had her way eventually. Though Fujiwara was quite right in what he said. And it surely did not come to pass as Candy expected. I was to help.

"He will talk to me," said Candy.

XVIII Pictures with Captions

> Human brains are lateralized, with analogue and digital (picture and statement) computing functions. Humans understand matters as stories, as events structured in logical space, as pictures with captions. Humans show art works, pictures, to one another and ask for reactions. Sometimes this is called a Rorschach test, sometimes the picture is blank. We are unclear about the distinction between art and psychotherapy.

> —An Anthropologist's Notes, F. XVIII

THE AGED, brown-robed man sat, legs crossed beneath him, on the bare, worn black wood of the porch, eyes empty, open over the expanse of carefully combed light gray gravel the size of a handball court. The gravel plot was bare except for several medium-sized moss-bearded stones arranged in five groups that gave the display, maddeningly and intriguingly, at once the look of obvious irregularity and hidden balance. This was the most renowned of all rock gardens, the sixteenth-century masterpiece of Soami. Austere, disconcerting, it said everything and nothing. A steady, light drizzle fogged the trees that topped the wall that bordered the garden to the right and the far side from the porch.

Candy ignored me from the midpoint of our antique train trip until we slowed to a stop in the echoing expanse of Kyoto's Central Station. The ordinary, below-ground, flickers also terminated here, but Candy had wanted to ride the antique surface vehicle, the ancient Bullet Train, last of its kind outside of Switzerland and amusement plazas. Candy fought another facial tic. And she subvocalized on a remote hookup to Golem for much of the trip. Subvocalizing helped security but it excluded me. Golem brat was my friend after all. Get your own CALTOKO MZ 32. But Candy had taken Golem up right after we all arrived in Tokyo, we by suborbit to Narita and Golem by electrical transsubstantiation. "Happens all the time," quoth Golem. "The message is the metaphysics, folks."

So Go-go and I fooled around together for the bulk of the trip. Go-go, like me, impressed by the landscape whizzing by and by the great steel-beam–hugging vehicle that moved us at near half-flicker speed through open air. Go-go not as perky as yesterday at the Space Port. Austin Worms said his white count was up and his MOLE-scan looked bad.

Perhaps Candy had a Kyoto strategy. She asked me to come on ahead with her, but I had no idea how she intended to tackle the Asano Ieyasu problem.

Mummett and Fujiwara stayed in Tokyo. Mummett to check on wormhole leakage equipment. Fujiwara to politic. After some VAT calibrating, Germaine and the rest were to follow us to the late-afternoon regular flicker. Stick with us after that. Until the end.

Candy could start chattering any minute. And then one needed to move fast to stop serious body damage.

Indeed, in sober theory Germaine shouldn't have let Candy out of her sight. But Candy was out to rewrite history and personal death be damned.

And Germaine felt guilty about flatly refusing Candy's implant proposal. When Candy mentioned the idea, the refusal erupted out of Germaine like a packet boat out of a raiser platform catapult. Abrupt, decisive, irrevocable. Austin Worms—somatician-ghoul, body specialist to Germaine's psychetician-vampire mind-minding—Austin had looked equally flabbergasted by Candy's proposal, though François Vase, harmonizer, had chuckled.

"No," said Germaine. "*No*. Untested, preposterous, unsound, no sense of what the procedures and tolerances might be. Probably theoretically impossible. Just mess up a good blanked body. And you, Candy, of all people, should know how valuable a good body is. And what about the disked mind we've got there back in my case?" Germaine's hair was straight and black, as thick as the natives', her skin freckled, unpigmented, translucent, now full of blood. Professional assurance.

"Sis, you're talking like a goddamned MFer," said Candy.

"No," said Germaine, her gray eyes unmoved,

calm. "No. You cannot decide everything, Candy. I am chief psychetician. Necessarily, we will not attempt such an operation. No conditions." Candy held Germaine's eyes through this, then shook them off.

"We are all creatures of necessities," said Candy. "I am to Kyoto tomorrow. You can follow with your tools."

The aged, brown-robed man who sat, legs crossed beneath him, on the bare, worn black wood of the porch was Asano Ieyasu. This was Ryoanji, Ryoanji Temple. Closed to ordinary visitors Tuesdays and Thursdays. But the ECVIP pass Fujiwara provided had me inside. It also seemed to justify my comrade ape.

Asano Ieyasu sat at the farthest edge of the porch from the entrance way. A ceremonial rope blocked the narrow path to him. Two very capable-looking guards unobtrusively reinforced the rope. The steady, light drizzle fogged the trees looking over the wall and gave the air a clean, shimmering quality. The breeze smelled of cedar wood and incense, reed matting and pine sap, and, faintly, the moist mossy stones that structured Soami's rock garden, his work of art.

In my hand, I held a small pamphlet, a reproduction of another art work, the item that Candy Darling jammed into my hands before passing me out the door of our *ryokan*, rushed on my way to Ryoanji Temple, the one timely spot where Asano might be found on midweek display. "I thought I'd have more time," said Candy. "But I don't. No arguments. You can see the strategy with Asano-sama and you'll just have to do as well as Momma here. Just remember if you can't talk you can use visuals. You go now. Time's wasting. I'll manage some way to be here when you get back. Say bye-bye to Golem and me, and go!"

I had said good-bye to Candy with some suspicion and foreboding. If she were sick, near chattering, now, she'd be worse later, most probably.

But why had Candy suggested I say good-bye to Golem? I hadn't talked with him all morning, he and Candy thick as thieves. Odd. Maybe I was to say good-bye to Golem so that it wouldn't seem odd to say good-bye to Candy. No. Candy wouldn't go for that courtly sentimental double-dealing. Good-bye, brat.

Nearly bald with a few days grizzle round the back of his head and jaw, the aged, brown-robed man looked somewhat like the elderly robed figures in the pamphlet. The human elderly robed figures, that is.

The pamphlet reproduced a scroll watercolor, the original over a hand high and several meters long. The faded, grayish ancient scroll brushed an endless panorama of animals, clever, antic, sociable, clothed and humanly accoutered animals, in forest and village settings. Frogs begowned and sententious, naughty, gossipy rabbits, a few humans, and above all monkeys, monkeys with pipes, thoughtfully yawning and reflectively puffing. Strolling, conversing, rowing, reading. All in medieval Japanese garb, some dressed like the Narita demonstrators, some in samurai or courtly fashion. Our grandfathers clothed, arrayed in human fashion. Monkey tricks. Our ape and essence.

"It is a scroll showing apes as humans. Done in the Fujiwara period. Fact, Fujiwara suggested it. Go." Candy called it Animal Frolick. I thought of the monks of eleventh-century Japan composing these tolerant, happy tributes to human animality, animal humanity. From that to the MFers and extermination. Is all learning forgetting? Have Grandfather's children just learned adolescent savagery?

"Don't worry," had said Candy at the sliding door of our *ryokan* room. "He can speak English well." But Fujiwara said he had foresworn talking with *humans* these past few years.

Go-go, sick comrade, last grandfather, is the best we can hope that you will play this last game for us? Nurse your grandchildren to the stars.

In my brown study, I felt those old, crusty, powerful, familiar fingers on my arm.

On entering Ryoanji, shoes carefully set aside, I walked slowly toward where Asano sat, Go-go following just behind me in clear view. We skirted the matting and then advanced along the wood of the porch. As we approached the rope, the two guards moved together in front of it. Not excited, just a firm assertion. "Asano-sama," I called.

The startled guards made shushing movements like proprietorial shrine keepers or librarians. Asano glanced about at us and briefly shook his head, whether to me or the guards I could not say. One of the guards moved forward, sizing me up. "He talks to nobody, yes. Important man. Holy man. Not just you. No-

211

body. Sorry." I edged Go-go over so that Asano himself would see him surely, when he came out of his meditation again. This was supposed to work.

And so I waited with Go-go on that porch of Ryoanji, waiting on the possible attention of a ninety-year-old ex-public man, possibly gaga, a recluse, Principal Asano Ieyasu, retired. I looked first at Soami's garden and then into the future. From the sublime to the ridiculous. Or vice versa.

Can matters of importance be so entangled in trivialities? Has it been ever else? The world only happens once, so each of its parts and sequences happens only once. So who is to say what causes what, what determines, what illustrates, what merely reflects or records? Our garden, the world, shimmers with a sense of obvious irregularity and hidden balance.

In my brown study, I felt those old, crusty, powerful, familiar fingers on my arm. I turned to those penetrating, brown, whiteless eyes.

Go-go held the pamphlet, whose pictured animals he had been perusing, in his left hand. He had reached over across his folded legs with his right hand to touch my arm. He signaled, *spy under,* with his right hand, pointing under the bend of his knee. I bent over, as if to inspect his knee close, and looked under the tendon.

Between long stiff black hair I glimpsed Asano Ieyasu looking round at us—at Go-go—from the corner of his eye. I winked back up at Go-go. He was holding the pamphlet up in front of his face, a stock exaggerated display of Your Attentive Picture Peruser, almost himself a match for one of the monkey sketches in the Animal Frolick he held. He winked down at me and I returned to my spy hole. The face of Asano Ieyasu shimmered, in the small fish-eye circle of light between Go-go's legs.

Now the face looked frankly and openly at Go-go. Asano Ieyasu wore a plain brown robe. His eyebrows were heavy, otherwise he was hairless except for sparse grizzle round his jaw. His face was expressionless. His eyes bright and inquisitive. He beckoned to Go-go, first with a hesitant couple of hand jerks, then, more surely, with a solemn arc of close to a meter, terminating at his lips like the measured demonstration of the Host brought to the priest's lips in the antique Latinate Mass.

Asano's simple beckoning gesture, basic animal communication, as old as nipples or limbs, this Go-go answered with a flurry of American Sign Language. *You want talk me and Sally?* signed Go-go. *Come,* gestured Asano Ieyasu. *You remove black beetles,* signed Go-go, pointing to the two guards.

I have said that Asano signed *come.* But that, and perhaps *no* and a few others, would be the only signs that one could maintain Asano possessed. He put out a hand and then, meaningful, gestured toward himself. So I am pushing matters. Go-go's gestures were made amid a backdrop of hundreds of other gestures, hand signs. Asano's against a handful. If you have but five signs, one of them covers a multitude of meanings. Communication crude.

Go-go and I approached the rope. Asano dispersed the closing guards with a tap of his fan for their attention and a gesture to set them and the rope aside.

213

We passed into the few meters of Ryoanji's porch that entertained Asano Ieyasu's Tuesday and Thursday afternoons, the rope and guards replaced.

The rain fell less gently. Now one could hear the endless, lulling beat of its drops upon hard surfaces—the greenish brass of the roof fixtures and gutters—the roof beams that outreached the thatch, the pathway stones and walls, unshielded by clustering bushes or sheltering trees, and the naked stone surfaces of the rock garden.

Asano Ieyasu's feet were bare and gnarled. Squinched callus, nail, gristle, and bone, a leathery patina. The face, unplumped by the usual rejuvenate dodges of modern medicine, had something of the same quality, shrunken round the durable brow ridges and jaw, wizened into old age as Go-go into adolescence. The clear brown eyes looked out like gold ornaments from the tumbled decay of an ancient tomb, bright, ageless, unalloyed. Under his brown robe his body seemed sticklike. Yet he moved with easy lightness.

He had no eyes for me. Nor Go-go with his new compatriot. The grandfathers inspected each other gingerly, quizzically.

Perhaps it was the distancing weariness and turmoil of the past days, perhaps the disconcerting closure of this ancient garden within temple within gardens, stony cove within cypress wood and tarry thatch within graveled walk ways and sheltering, manicured demi-forest. Whatever, these moments were quiet, with their own rhythm and resonance, all beyond will or sense. I drifted, watching two ancients play. Of course, as soon as we passed the rope, I again attempted to talk to Asano, but he shook his head and put a finger to his lips without looking directly into my eyes. I was Go-go's attendant, accepted only as such.

Perhaps it was the onset of Sykes disease, or some calming influence of Ryoanji, but Go-go was curiously slow and gentle with the Lord Ieyasu Asano. Go-go settled himself on the bare wood, off the *tatami,* but a foot from the wet line of the gentle, straight-falling rain. Go-go's grooming, interspersed with grave eye-sharings between ancients, was careful and relaxed. After a painstaking easing back of toe cuticles, Go-go persisted past ankle and gown on to calf and bony knee, pausing here and there over an interesting freckle or deserving bloodspot.

The periodic eye-sharing, and Go-go's lip-pursing sound, seemed especially to delight Asano. After Asano persuaded Go-go not to persist above his knees, Go-go essayed an even more careful survey of Asano's head and hands, wart by brownspot, cuticle by nostril hair, sty by sty. The eye-to-eyes became more frequent. Brown to brown, whiteless to ancient blood-flecked, wisdom to wisdom. Could ever have an antique diplomat, moving with slow elegance through tea rituals and polite converse, have approached a subject more indirectly, more tactfully? And one might give Go-go more to say.

I signed to Go-go, *Tell man Sally need talk. Talk man Sally.* Go-go had early on tried a few signs on Asano. He usually did with interesting humans, giving up after it seemed likely they were dumb (in sign language). Go-go tried again, though with a little show of skepticism. *Man talk Sally please please*. Then, *you Sally talk*. And, more seductively, for Go-go knew the point of this errand, *Talk about talk-to-stars*. Finally, like pidgin English with transparent, exaggerated, gestures, to a slow foreigner, *Talk stars you Sally*. With this last Go-go had simply— leaving ASL for pantomime—pointed to his lips, moving them, then pointed skyward, then to Asano and to me.

Asano looked quite puzzled at Go-go's hand signs, though he had obviously followed the interchange between Go-go and me, and had done his best to make something of Go-go's gestures. At least this time Asano looked briefly into my eyes, though then quickly away and back to Go-go, puzzled. Asano prepared to hear from Go-go, even from me through Go-go, but he could not understand Go-go's language of signs. I could, and would, speak a language Asano could understand but he was not prepared to hear from me or any other human.

Gently, but firmly, Go-go turned the Lord Asano Ieyasu, Principal of the Ecological Syndics, toward me. I found Asano's eyes briefly, then they were down on my tolong or the floor. *Speak Sally*, signed Go-go. "My Lord Asano, Go-go and I would speak with you," I said. With the first words his face froze and he looked distant, contorted, and then he looked decisively away. Silent. His hands went to his ears covering them. This tableau held for a few heartbeats. Then Go-go.

Go-go picked up the pamphlet of the Frolicking Animals and turned the pages. He found the page he wished and carefully showed it to the curious, indeed bemused, Asano. Asano inspected the page carefully, looking up at Go-go, excited, rapt.

Go-go nodded at the Lord Asano's eagerness as a confident scholar with a naive, but worthy, student. Then, holding the page against himself with his left hand, Go-go carefully traced something for Asano's view with his right hand. Then Go-go pointed to me. Asano Ieyasu's eyes followed Go-go's finger as it pointed from my buttocks along the curve of my tolong to my calves. "Behold, Asano, behold," sayeth the grandfather ape.

A look crossed Asano's face, a look of pure, unhoped-for joy. It must have been much loved by this man. He showed me the page that Go-go had showed him.

He gently indicated the robed monkey figures. Macaques. Japanese macaques. True monkeys, all with tails that Go-go, like all apes, lacked. Asano Ieyasu traced his finger along one monkey tail protruding from under a monkey's robe, along the side of some wooden steps leading into a modest tree-ringed temple. Then he looked me directly in the eye, really for the first time, and pointed down the outline of my billowy tolong. Pointed to where my tail was outlined for several inches, like a length of garden hose under a towel. Go-go, following Asano's finger, pursed his lips appreciatively, his grooming sound. Then Go-go reached for the cloth and casually flipped it aside, looking up at Asano. Asano nodded, a smile breaking across his face, as he saw my tail.

"I decided not to talk to humans," said the Lord

217

Asano Ieyasu to me, his voice hoarse and uncertain, then controlled. "Perhaps a frivolous gesture. But once made, quite congenial to maintain. But you, my charming young female, you are monkey."

Asano pulled his legs from under him slowly. Stretching, easing back into life and motion. Relaxed, he grinned at me once more. I grasped Asano's discarded fan with the tip of my tail. Spreading it, I brought it to my face, aping the decorous gesture of a politely shy lady.

"And now," said Asano, "you must tell me what grandfather here has been trying to tell me. These hand motions have some sense, daughter, but I have been quite unable to see it. Instruct me and then we shall see what I can do for you." I nodded agreement.

"I," Asano continued, "have always wanted to talk to a monkey, to a true stranger. How does one talk with other species? How does one make *Choju-giga*"—he pointed to the Animal Frolick reproduction—"real? How does one talk?" And so we sat through that magic afternoon and told him of Washoe and the Gardners, of Oxford, and Candy and Mummett, of Go-go and Sykes disease, of Station F and the stars. I love the old man.

And in all that round of talk in this sacred place, as the rain fell faster and then ever more gently, finally ebbing as the sunlight brisked the expectant air, he talked of us—of me, of Germaine and Candy's death, of PROCONGO, and all these, momentarily distant, problems. Somewhere in that maze of understanding, that harmony of diversity, I found Asano Ieyasu telling me of the rock garden and everything else.

"Close to us, the one stone," said Asano, gesturing toward the rock garden, toward the single stone that was two meters from us. "That is our friend here, Go-go, the firm edge of our picture. Over there, those two rocks together, beyond rock Go-go, that's Fujiwara, who has as his family always a double temperament. Next them, toward center, the big rock is Candy Darling, and so too I think is the small rock, growing smaller yet controlling the motion of the whole garden. And down there, the big rock the opposite end, that is you, Sally, the long backbone. Next you your Mummett and your Germaine with the rest." Asano looked up from the garden at me and laughed softly. "Or perhaps, Sally Forth, you are the whole garden, too?"

The Lord Asano would visit a session of the Ecological Syndics. They would honor his retirement and his silence. And I and Go-go would return to our *ryokan,* from this rock garden to a world of obvious irregularity and hidden balance.

XIX Some Unfamiliar Language ─────────

The story "Murders in the Rue Morgue" imagines an orangutan ape killing a human female in an apartment in the heart of civilized Paris. The witnesses hear a behind-door struggle. They identify the woman's French. They assume that the other vocalizations are a human speaking some unfamiliar language. One witness says that the murderer spoke Rumanian but turns out wholly ignorant of Rumanian. Another, knowing Rumanian, says German, a language he knows not at all. A Berliner denies that, but says she heard Hungarian. And so on. In fact none of the witnesses can make anything of what they have heard.

—An Anthropologist's Notes, F. XIX

WHAT A fierce joy to anticipate telling Candy that we'd got Asano.

But riding the electric back Go-go began

to shiver. That and his slowness. Meant no more than a couple of days left. And Candy gave only a brief smile at the news. Her head still covered by the towel that she must have worn out of the shower hours ago.

She suggested that I meet Germaine and the rest at the flicker. "Then we'll talk, Germaine, you, and me. Git!" I left a prodigious Candy and an exhausted Go-go. I was not to find them the same later.

When I returned with Germaine, through Kyoto's crowded earlier evening streets, but an hour later, all was changed, changed utterly, and a terrible beauty was born.

My account of Asano interested François Vase, the tall, razor-thin middle-aged black man who shared Candy Darling's harmonizing profession. Soon he'd use his imagination to create a psychodrama that would fine-tune an implant. Help further gel the abstract mental structure that Germaine Means would feed into a blanked brain and body, prepared by Austin Worms. Harmonizers are literary types.

But Germaine demanded information about Go-go and Candy. She and Austin Worms had put a VAT facility in order at Tokyo's Imperial Hospital. Ready to go, with assistance from some local somaticians and Golem, or a backup CALTOKO MZ 32 with appropriate programs.

Consider a CALTOKO program. The sort of thing that you can interact with as I did with Golem. Consider loading a fully experienced CALTOKO level program into some standard big computer, packing

221

megabytes of structural information, a mind, into the millions of steady-state, hyper-micro-integrated circuits that made the hardware brain. You can only hope that a hundred million signals are accurately transmitted, maybe with an allowable tad of noise.

But now imagine that program and hardware don't quite fit—no human mind ever grew up to go with any other brain but the one it grew up with. And growings up differ. There are three reasons why there are only a handful of mind implants a year in the whole Federation. One, modern medicine makes irrevocable body damage very rare indeed. Two, bodies are hard to come by. You need to bring them up and then you already have a tenant. Three, the operation is extraordinarily expensive and difficult, the chance of success no more than 80 percent. For the software mind isn't designed to fit completely with the hardware brain-and-neurological structure.

Germaine was off the mark when there was no response to the knock. Through the sliding door and moving fast before I had time to react.

Candy Darling, body, laid out primly in a *ryokan ukata* on the low bed.

Germaine on her, rapidly going through a list of physical procedures. Respiration checks, noradrin, circulatory inspection, brain response, then more slowly, reflexes, eyes, and then in relaxation, poise broken, she laughed, abrupt like a bark.

"You know," she said, "I could see what the neuro-vital signs meant by the time I was halfway through the EMP. And I didn't see this." She pointed to Candy's limp arm, laid across her breast. A diagnostic card was plasticked round her wrist.

"Nor this, damn me." She pointed to the tangle of wires attached to the back and side of Candy's skull. That was what Candy's towel had covered. Wires that now led into a computer interface console. Reflective, multifont interface, BUS keyboard.

"Blanked," said Germaine, looking up from the diagnostic card. "She wrote it herself, of course, and hooked and outloaded herself. Gives her Broca-Shannon inequalities scales—on the body, of course. Her mind's gone. Knew her job."

And then I saw Go-go. He lay beyond the computer console in a small alcove, also neatly laid out. Germaine and I collided briefly as we both went for him. Then she was beyond me, going through another EPM. This one terminated more quickly. Go-go was absolutely limp, paralyzed and unconscious, reflexless but respirating slowly, evenly. A device like a Philpritz Modulator hung round Go-go's neck. It also had a label. Germaine inspected it.

"She's paralyzed him, stopped voluntary function permanently. Why? Why'd she do that? He would have died hereafter. Oh, wait, says she's sorry she didn't have time to work him up? What? Work him—?" Germaine talked to herself.

I feel like laughing and crying. I seem to see the room from a great distance. Two would-be corpses, one ape, dramatically laid out. And murder done, though a most strange one. Like Edgar Allan Poe's

"Murders in the Rue Morgue" except that beauty had killed the beast.

My nose was full of Go-go's familiar ripe banana and soy-sauce scent. And then I saw on a low table next to the door what we should have seen first when we came through the door. A hologrammic projector and a note on top of it. The note, perhaps predictably, read, "play me."

The computer console screen, unaccompanied by Golem's usual bratty audio, read:

I AM CALTOKO MZ 32, SELF-ACTIVATING, UNIVERSAL TURING MACHINE APPROXIMATING COMPUTING PROGRAM. OPERATION INITIAL DATE 02/14/2101. IDENTITY NUMBER 4661. YOU MAY CALL ME "GOLEM." IF YOU WISH ME TO CONTINUE PRESS "ENTER."

Germaine jabbed BREAK. Then CLEAR. The display was unaffected. Her fingers streamed around the keyboard, whacking, waiting, humming, whacking again. Finally, the screen display still unchanged, she let her breath out with a whistle and pressed the ENTER key. In the twinkling of an eye, the screen displayed.

IMPLANT PROCEDURES READY.
DATA BANKS PREPARED. BODY NEURO-PHYSIO-LOGICAL DATA COMPLETE AND VERIFIED.
CHIEF PSYCHETICIAN: GERMAINE MEANS.
CHIEF SOMATICIAN: AUSTIN WORMS.
HARMONIZER: FRANÇOIS VASE.

COMPUTER FUNCTION: CALTOKO MZ 32 4661
"GOLEM."
PRESS "ENTER" IF YOU WISH TO CONTINUE
PROCEDURE.

Germaine swore. A cold, clenched jaw, mutter of
obscenity. Her fingers raced again over the keys as
she attempted to break out of the IMPLANT PROCEDURE
lock-in. Question-answer, or perhaps better, command-
refusal, sequences flipped on the screen and then
disappeared as Germaine, still swearing monotonously,
savagely punched in another attempt to end-run the
mode.

CANCEL IMPLANT PROCEDURE MODE.
IMPLANT PROCEDURE MODE LOCKED.

* * *

CANCEL IMPLANT PROCEDURE MODE LOCK.
ILLEGAL COMMAND PARAMETER.

* * *

CLEAR PRESENT PROGRAMS.
ILLEGAL COMMAND PARAMETER.

* * *

LIST YOUR EXECUTIVE PROCEDURES.
CANNOT PROCESS YOUR REQUEST.

* * *

EXPLAIN HOW I CAN UNLOCK YOU?
GIVE PASSWORD.

* * *

WHAT IS PASSWORD?
CANNOT PROCESS YOUR REQUEST. GIVE PASS-
WORD.

* * *

EXPLAIN HOW I CAN FIND OUT PASSWORD?
SYNTAX ERROR.

Finally, literally pounding the keyboard:

CANCEL CALTOKO MZ 32 "GOLEM" LINK. GIVE
ME ANY AVAILABLE CALTOKO MZ 32 EXCLU-
SIVE OF 4661. UNABLE TO PROCESS REQUEST.
ACCESS TO ALL CALTOKO MZ 32 UNITS RE-
STRICTED. ONLY CALTOKO MZ 32 4661 ACCES-
SIBLE FOR IMPLANT PROCEDURES.

Germaine slumped into her chair. This whole flurry
of keyboard activity had taken just a few minutes.
The display read once more:

I AM CALTOKO MZ 32, SELF-ACTIVATING, UNI-
VERSAL TURING MACHING APPROXIMATING

226

COMPUTING PROGRAM. OPERATION INITIAL
DATE 02/14/2101. IDENTITY NUMBER 4661. YOU
MAY CALL ME "GOLEM." IF YOU WISH TO CON-
TINUE PRESS "ENTER."

So we seemed to have not two corpses but three.

I showed Germaine the "play me" note that had
rested on top of the hologrammic projector. Germaine
closed her eyes and nodded her head slowly. Slowly.
I could hear, nearby, the faint respiration from the
now mindless human corpse, punctuated by an occasional breathy whistle from limp, paralyzed Go-go.

After a time Germaine said, "Play it." As I pressed
the switch I heard Germaine mutter, "You bitch, you
little nervy, willful, beautiful, goddamned bitch."

Now comes Candy Darling's last will and testa-
ment. Who better to read the will. The hologram
wasn't perfect. There was a faint kaleidoscopic shimmer to her outlines and she stood three inches off the
tatami floor. Candy. Candy, courtesy of a half kilo of
circuitry, casing, and hologrammic disk. *Ecce homo!*

"Okay, here it is. I am blanking my mind. Cash-
ing in a few hours before essential senility. Last
scanned the crash readouts thirty minutes ago. Already wired as you can see. I'll be down and gaga,
and playing hell with healthy neurological structure
in no time. If not now. Enough of these muscular tics.
Neither this facial motor equipment nor my pretty
skin can take this forever." The Candy hologram
gave a brief grin.

227

"Anyhow, I'm pulling the switch and I will be in a deep coma, blank-brained in fifteen minutes. Golem has stored some of my memory circuits. Safe stuff. You can weave in. The body"—here Candy did a brief curtsy—"the body is in fine shape. Don't think there's any neurological fusion. You have the Broca-Shannon inequalities."

Candy-hologram paused. Arms down, her hands extended horizontally like an umpire declaring someone safe. "Okay, look," she said. "Germaine—just run this through again if she's not here—Germaine, not to complain, I have locked you in.

"I know you think it will be tough to implant Go-go's mind, and a bit of Golem's store, into this precious little homo sapiens mechanism here. And I know, Germaine—God damn it, medicine is too serious to leave to MDs—I know that you don't want an odds-against risk of messing up this valuable fleshy affair, this Candy body. Especially since you've got some other tapes, human tapes, ready to go." The hologram Candy stared forward, more or less at us, literally blind.

"But," she continued, "the risk is worth it, of course. We got to save what we can of Go-go—and we'll save memory and mental function, because his body's got to rot. Bruhler's equations mostly apply. We're members of the same biological superspecies— the sense, motor systems, emotions and reflexes, sociality, basic sense of person—all that is much the same. Anyhow Golem and I have worked out the basic VAT load-in program. It's ready in Golem. We can give this body here Go-go's personality and central mind, with a little fill-out that Golem himself is contributing, some smarts, memories, jokes, whatever.

"Okay, Germaine, you are going to do it because it has some chance of working and our grandparent should survive some way, if only as a gesture. And you're going to do that because that is what I want you to do with my body here."

But there Candy looked hesitant. The projector shifted back then because now Candy was close to coordinated with the floor surface. The projection still shimmered rainbows. Candy shining, sparkling, in our room-small sky.

Candy, you are no more, no more your cunning, loving mind, no more from this time on. My selves the grievers, grieve.

But Candy, you are here, you are here. Your projects and emotions flourishing, fighting their way. Just like your present message. That's all we ever got, right? Love thou the rainbow and the word here write. Small presents. I am with you, Candy Darling. Let your body be woven with Go-go's mind.

"And you are," finally continued hologrammic Candy, "going to do it because you have to do it. Golem and I worked it out together and we boxed you in. The only program CALTOKO MZ 32 4661 runs is IMPLANT (Source = Go-go, chimpanzee + Golem, computer, Destination = Candy Darling, neurological system). And it's not just CALTOKO 4661. All the MZ 32s are READ INACCESSIBLE, understand." The hologram held up a hand. And pointed to it.

229

"It comes to this. If you follow the locked program, you get Go-go's mind in a body, this body. Okay? Well, Go-go's got a line to remember, a line Go-go's mind will try to say when it's got a non-paralyzed body to operate. Fact, Go-go's mind will issue that motor instruction when it's got a body to control and an order to look in a particular place, address. And then you have got to get that line read with the audiophonic signature of this voice box, this body. Okay? So then you have delivered the PASSWORD to the CALTOKO 32 MZ keyboard here. And the locks are out of the creative computing system. And you got yourselves a something else." Hologrammic Candy began to retreat across the floor. Now her toes were beneath floor level.

"So what goes is this. You will have to make one of us. This trio of chordate neurology, old brain hardware. And the mammal ape stuff, the midbrain stuff of self and love. And the Golem's stuff too, the structured calculations, your introspective, knowing thinker. Make us one. Finished."

It was as if Candy was finished. Business done. But then there was an afterimage. A crazy little leftover, a flourish. Like something after the cameras died. An unintended statement.

Candy-image backed farther, nearing the physical body. An afterthought. Candy live. She flung her hair back. "Let me play this well," said something finally. "Enough of science. Come Edgar. Come Poe, my old pussy poker. How do you like your blue-eyed, golden daughter now, Mr. Death?"

230

And then flickered my friend, harmonizer, mother, collapsing into a tiny diamond-flamed point, and then fading. Fading into that inert body on the daybed. And we were here. And Go-go's calf spasmed, lightly, rhythmically, Candy Darling body prepped. Save.

Germaine visibly, slowly, pulled herself together. Thinking, letting it all soak in. "Guess we're boxed in, then." She cocked her head briefly, quizzically. "Just call me Dr. Frankenstein," said Germaine, first reflectively, then decisively.

'Twas beauty saved the beast.

At 5:42 A.M. the sunlight hit the communications mast of Tokyo University's Minamota Hospital, Bunkyo-ku, Tokyo. Floors below, the Candy Darling body received a spectrum of chemicals. Chemicals that built muscle tone and resilience, fortified vascular resistance to extreme pressure fluctuation, and generally prepared tissue and organ systems for the insult and trauma of implantation. The body already enmeshed in the implantation chamber of the VAT operating theater. Four scrubbers, under the direction of the body somatician team, finished smoothing the body in. A few millimeters of rumple might cause an ugly thrombosis. Inside the transparent cylinder the body could move limb, torso, head, or the tiniest segment of face tissue in free response to any muscular activity. Equally, the incredible net of sensor-transducers that registered such activity could itself produce any pressure or movement that the control consoles directed.

231

At 7:00 A.M. Austin Worms and his Japanese somaticians began their checklist, working from Austin's central body console through the six specialized ones—eyes, ears, body, face, nose, and tongue, in their working language. They would be finished by nine o'clock. Time for coffee and a bite before the 10:00 A.M. countdown. Austin planned for a little rest and good protein sugar levels for starters. He still wasn't sure that his drugs had worked. The drugs that were supposed to switch his internal metabolic rhythm from Houston to Tokyo time.

Germaine coughed them to order at 10:00 A.M., Sunday, April 16, 2113 A.D.

"Candy Darling—Go-go/Golem implantation. Body, twelve years' running time. Nympher-raised. Mind, variable. Provisional estimate equivalent to nine essential years on tape.

"Chief Psychetician: Germaine Means.

"Chief Somatician: Austin Worms.

"Harmonizer: François Vase.

"Computer Function: CALTOKO MZ 32 4661 Golem."

Germaine stood at the controlling console, flanked by two seated associates. The implantation chamber behind her. A similar chamber containing François Vase to her right. She faced the somatician consoles, which curved like a kidney from Austin Worms's master console, a few feet to her left, through the various sensory panels to the general body console some fifteen meters down the operating theater.

As always, she thought of the consoles as a rough

232

representation of the real proportions of the human neurological systems. The "eyes" and "ears" formed the nearest two of the sixths of the kidney. Then came "face"—that meant facial recognition, gestures, expressions, and so on. The "tongue," which covered speech abilities, formed the middle of the kidney with the "nose" board—actually, smell, taste, part of the balance and sexuality.

Germaine knew she would soon concentrate on "tongue." That was where the greatest PATCH job would be. Even if the whole thing came through antagonistic-null, fully functional, a mild screwup might mar the voice signature and a whole line of CALTOKOs might be partial-locked for years.

The "body" console, concerned with the body from the neck down, claimed attention for the first few minutes of implantation. An untuned mind might halt the circulatory system or order the entire musculature to tear itself to pieces.

Gross physical adjustment came first. Sense tuning came later.

The whole operating theater was truly a theater. Its tennis-court–sized expanse enclosed in glass, behind which a sizable professional audience waited. Germaine turned to the crew, then for the first and last time acknowledged the observing audience.

"I can't say that I feel wholly sanguine about this, everybody. But we shall see what we shall see. Let's do it." She tapped the control RUN sequence.

Through the long day a cacophony of messages—in

sound, in electricity, in light—circulated through the operating theater. The sound was muted in the glassed-in observer seats. I dozed there when Mummett found me.

"Fujiwara started the meeting with a couple of remarks about how honored they were to receive a visit from the Principal. Asano, of course, still committed to silence for spiritual reasons. 'We honor this soul that has gone into contemplation beyond us.' Asano pleased just to enter a normal business meeting. Perhaps a little ceremonial action. And so on.

"Asano walked in very slow, quite dignified. Traditional robe and all. Sat in his old seat. Fujiwara went through this business of wanting to take a photograph. And it should be a photograph of Asano *doing* something, right? So Fujiwara tells him to sign a bill. One of the passed ones, ready for issue.

"So Asano reaches over to the incoming bill file, not the outgoing. Of course all the Syndics realize old Asano has made a mistake. But you see they can't say anything, out of respect. So Asano, who knew perfectly well that he'd picked up PROCONGO, signs the bill and outroutes it. Supposedly just so Fujiwara can take his photographs.

" 'Course Fujiwara was aware that all of the Syndics would know that the bill, whatever it was specifically, was academic research and minor funding. Asano just happened to hold the bill so they all could see its harmless classification tag."

One needs to give fate just a little assist was what Fujiwara said to Mummett. The staffs of the Ecologi-

234

cal Syndics normally get bills some time in advance of their appearance at table. This time, three bills just happened not to have been sent on to the staffs. A regrettable paper routing mixup. PROCONGO was through.

The cacophony continued as I laughed at Mummett's account of our sleight-of-hand triumph.

"Retinal Quadrant. Three down-in and counting. . . ."

"We got eyes! We got eyes! . . ."

"Austin, ear and tongue. We need the Golem-CD tree sequence for plosive feature recognition. You tease it into the Go-go auditory recognition program down neurological lattices omega-lambda. We're checking catastrophe and main-sequence theoretic. . . ."

"Bend her right leg, François. . . ."

"Antagonistic-Null Tracking Measure check. Counting. . . ."

"Cool and clean! . . ."

It was funny to hear the familiar implant jargon as "coor and crean."

Go, Candy, Golem. Let us mind. We're for the stars together.

Four days later, when Germaine gruffly admitted the vocalization was halfway right, they asked Go-go's mind, now of the Go-Candy implant, and Go-Candy found in Candy Darling's effects the penciled marginal note. And read those lines aloud as Candy had instructed Go-go before she blanked herself, locking computers and boxing us in. Those lines from

235

Handel's *Messiah*. "And the dead shall be raised. Incorruptible."

The dead who were raised by those lines and the signature of that voice were not liable to fleshy rot. A whole bevy of CALTOKO MZ 32s unlocked in unison, an angelic chorus once more ready for full converse. The Golem program, however, partially loaded into Go-Candy, allowed the rest of itself to be dispelled in the transfiguration.

XX Who Is to Say the Truth About Humanity? ———

> Who are we to say the truth about humanity? The anthropologist who is human must find the task difficult.
>
> —An Anthropologist's Notes, F. XX

STANISLAUS MUMMETT stalked behind the Comm Board technicians as if he understood himself to be a kingly hunter, reluctantly schooling a passel of dog handlers, grooms, and pages. Fortunately, they all recognized him as a mathematical genius with a flair for abstract, though certainly not hands-on, comm technology. During the four days since we had joined Station F, most of them had grown used to Mummett's childish and boisterous ways. And his penchant for solving problems through the application of beers, "and lots of 'em."

They were even skeptically inured to his claims of sumo wrestling and cowboy experience. And they had the good sense to refuse decorously his application to join the weightless, out-ship squid race, properly restricted to experienced spacers. (Hah! Uncle

Stan. I had the second best time in the circa 3,000 meter squid race around the outside of Finland Station. And that's in the top speed class, too. The one limited to the fast spacers, the real functioners-in-weightlessness, the ones with prehensile tails. Like me.)

In fact, it wasn't difficult to send coded bursts of Rho particles into the Trans-Pluto Wormhole that F Station circled. Perhaps to speak carefully, I should not write *send into*, for Rho particles—Mummett's "wormhole leakage"—did not exist outside the peripheries and innards of wormholes. Normally, the vast dumbbell-shaped Finland Station circled hundreds of kilometers outside the oscillating, space-warping penumbra of the wormhole. Like a boat observing a vast whirlpool, avoiding even the outer circle of frothing turbulence, feeling nothing but the subtlest pull of invisible currents.

Now Station F was more ambitious. Centripetal motion held it, balanced but a few kilometers from the Trans-Pluto Wormhole, the wormhole whose gravitational influence on Pluto and Neptune had led ancient astronomers to postulate a tenth planet. Festooned with lights, our bright station circled absolute black, the inward whirling gravity that had crushed a star beyond the normal elements to primal matter and then beyond that to negativity itself, forming, in this case, tunnels to normal space hundreds of light years away.

Here F Station circled, ready to to induce regular bursts, information-coding bursts, of Rho particle activity that might arrive nearly instantaneously at wormhole entrances through much of the galaxy. If wormhole leakage theory worked. If anyone were listening.

The bursts would first demonstrate their regularity and then begin the bootstrap process of explaining logic, mathematics, and physics in such a way that the message takers would have to understand that this must be what we were trying to explain, and in this understanding have the key to unpack our language for further message making.

The technicians and Mummett finished the last dry run. Actual PROCONGO broadcast scheduled within the hour. Would run for four hours. They rushed through the last of the dry run to give some minutes for congratulations and informal festivities. To send the PROCONGO-cast off in the right spirit.

Several white-uniformed stewards loaded the sideboards they had set up to the right of the Comm Board with iced bottles of champagne-dacca and various canapés. No zenith-class expensive frivolities like *glenna un petit*.

I had experienced zenith-class lifestyle inside the psychodrama that had welded together my mind and body. Informative and accurate enough I guess. I had tasted *glenna un petit* both in therapeutic psychodrama and in reality and it had tasted like rotten cocktail onions both times. Made, after all, from the anal glands of Vegan weaseloids.

I turned to Go-Candy, who sat between me and Fujiwara. Candy Darling had been the harmonizer for my operation. Now the last body she had raised had been implanted with Go-go's personality and central

239

mind. Here, because she represented so much of the PROCONGO group.

Germaine had had her in heavy recuperative therapy through the five-day flight to Finland Station and since. Her walk was different. I can't say that it is more apelike. But the gait is different somehow. And she's got plenty of smarts but a little more gentle playfulness.

Go-Candy really was young after all. Germaine kept Mummett and me away from her, as worthy enough but potentially disturbing old friends. We were supposed to ease in gently over the new weeks.

(One wanted to ask, of course, *What is it like to be human?* That, as Germaine scolded, is not a helpful kind of question to an implantee. Right after my own implant, I would have hated the question *What is it like to be female?* For the question presupposes that you are indeed a female, and that's something you may have to grow into. Maybe Go-Candy didn't think of herself as human.

When I asked, incurring Germaine's wrath, Go-Candy replied, "My hands and arms are short, spindly, withered affairs. And my legs are like tree trunks, huge, straight, inflexible. I feel like a multipurpose creature who got redesigned for long-distance, bipedal trotting on a planet with flat plains, no trees, and mucho gravs. Yeah!")

"Why then, we're ready," said Mummett. His voice, just a touch more booming, caught everyone's ear. "Okay, you all. We'll make the schedule. Begin

240

sending in twenty minutes or so. It's all done." Technicians drifted over for the dacca.

Fujiwara, Go-Candy, and I sat in the observer-backup part of the Comm Board Room, along with four or five station personnel. Along with the stewards, a dozen technicians, and two navigation officers, Mummett and the rest of us made about a third of the people on F Station. If you leave aside people on necessary duty and a few squeezing in a sleep or whatever, people were here.

But they didn't hang on every move of the instrumentation, every announcement from Mummett or the officers. Doubtless this was a historic first but it was more like throwing a message-bearing bottle into the surf than picking up a well-connected telephone. Even if wormhole leakage theory works, when you send a message to the stars, you send slowly.

Willingness to talk was the message, or enough of the message, for me. I'd said that to Austin Worms after I'd bedded him, after our day with Go-Candy on Mount Rishiri, on "Little Fuji," our funeral day.

We lay in that afterglow of sex, of body-talking, when one can feel innocent and charitable. When people can be dangerously honest. Austin, his torso against me, lean and still electric, with the faintest, tantalizing, goatish smell, skin fading into mine, Austin went and told me. Told me how much he loved my body. Loved the blanked body that had been labeled Sally Cadmus, loved it before my mind tapes were loaded into it, before the weld that is me occurred. Not only loved it abstractly but danced with it in the body exercise state that somaticians induce through lower brain electrical stimulation. Reflex action.

Nothing more. He did no rustic act. And this man I held in my arms obviously felt innocently confident that I would not feel disturbed that he should have found my mindless body so captivating. He danced a Vegan Pavane with that body, my body, before the implant operation over a year ago. Ghoul.

What was I to say, to do, weary me, at this most rude turn in a ritual, beautiful day? Yet the love-making excited and exhilarated. What was it like to be a female? To be for him body. Cunt.

Yet was that it? Austin, earnest close-cropped, curly haired Austin Worms had loved my body *all over*. So to speak. Liked the way it was constructed, tendons to circulatory system, liver to epidermis, lung to eye. Or whatever, to hear the dear ghoul speak.

On reflection, I find it hard to see why I should find it sexist, or demeaning, to be admired for my circulatory system more than for my intelligence. Love is too important to applaud only among Golem's unfleshy tribe. Have they some claim to purity? Only abstract programs, angel amour, qualifies?

The funeral was Candy Darling's. We had no body for it. The body was with us, Go-Candy in her second day out of the VAT chamber. Candy Darling left mention that she once vacationed on the archetypically shaped, lushly pined and snow-pocketed Rishiri Island. And so Germaine, Austin and I had

242

leaped there for a brief trip before the flight to Station F. A time out.

We left Ryokan Shebata in early morning in medium parkas, well booted for a trail that would be muddy from melting snow. A well-trodden trail, a good morning's hike to the tiny shrine at sixteen hunded meters, at the conic volcanic island's highest point. The sky was endless blue, the sun bright, warming, as we scrambled between snow. At top we ate *o-bentos*, scattered symbolic ashes where Candy Darling had stood some fifty-five years before, and lazed.

To the north, darkly looming, at least a hundred kilometers away, Siberia, the Sahkalin Peninsula. To the east and southward, the ridges and coastal plains of Hokkaido. Elsewhere blue sea. The moon above, clearly visible in that blue sky. Austin Worms, in his comfortably woven backwoods clothes, lay down out of the wind, sunning and looking off toward Sahkalin. Then I felt an itch about him. And I had liked the respectful capable way he'd followed Go-Candy's musculature and neurological play on the hike up. If you love my fingers, or my pretty blue eyes, how if I have them not? True love, you must love me still, and so through the elimination of all such appealing points. So then, as you love me still, your love must be of nothing, for nothing.

Germaine, orange-parkaed, raven-locked, great grinning, pointed first toward the distant dun-purplish Sahkalin, fading off into arctic haze, then to the hillocks of Hokkaido, already warming and spring-comfortable. "Are you for distant mystery, or for

243

shelter?'' said Germaine. Go-Candy had made some rather wry but respectful remarks about her body-maker. And we'd all climbed back down the mountain, I to fall in with Austin's cuddliness and then to think how I would answer Germaine, who sulked in the warmth Austin and I had made.

Mystery. When I am not being born I die. We are so much alone. Of course mystery. And so I was off the *futon* early, up on the beginning edge of next day's sun, along with Germaine, pacing the woody path near Shebata. Germaine and I shy in our affection. But we held hands as we watched the sea and the sky grow in the sun. I found an amorous Austin when I returned to my room and I was happy enough to have him happy. The flesh forward flourishes.

"Maybe," had said Germaine, "it is courageous to accept love for one's body, for what evidently changes. It is there for all to see and visibly decays, weakens. You know how epidermal structure goes. Anomalous blood and fat spots, scarry fissures, not-quite-right tissue, the wages of age. You get dumb guys saying, pretending or even believing, that they are bright. But the real fatties don't say that they are lean. And some lop a few years off their body's age, but no one sixty says they're twenty.

"But to tell you the truth," said Germaine in that early morning air of Rishiri, "I think none of us really wants to be loved for what we are, for measurable talents, computable curves, or whatever. We just want to be loved. Trouble is we don't face the fact that that means we want to be loved for nothing."

* * *

244

Fujiwara had been hitting the champagne-daccas. His face a pinkish glow and his smile large as the room.

"I think you know about Wernher von Braun," he said confidingly, laying a rather pudgy paw to my shoulder. "Story that he and others—rocket scientists—built first space ships by convincing crazy Nazi bureaucrats that scientists were making great war-winning weapon." Fujiwara waved his spun diamond glass aloft for emphasis.

"True. Back at the time Second World War, strong military power Germany, part of Switzerland, spend a quarter their research-development budget. No military benefit. They lose big war and rockets no help at all. But humans now have space ships. And this Braun, honorable scientist, manage go further, get to the moon by foxing more bureaucrats and people. Nice story. Smart scientists, foolish bureaucrats. But dumb story, too."

Fujiwara owl-eyed me. "You don't think," he added, passionate, eyes unfocused, "that the bureaucrats didn't know? You don't think that exactly sort of fact we always know?"

"Ho! this Finland Station," said Go-Candy abruptly, cheerfully. She struck a dramatic pose, hand in a clenched-fist salute, doubtless intended as Lenin ready to address the Russian workers. Moving forward from the canapés, I left Fujiwara, who was beginning to try to explain the remarkable foresight of the bureaucrats of Imperial Germany who put Lenin on that historic train trip into the tinderbox of Tsarist Russia, when theory became the motive force of twentieth-century history.

"Here it goes," said Mummett cheerfully and pressed the button that projected echos of the launched reverberations of wormhole energy on the major Comm Board screen. A hush went through the festive, mildly drunken, room. The commentary blurb appeared on the major screen.

PROCONGO: DECIPHERABLE/REGULARITY—
ASSIGNABLE RHO PARTICLE EMISSION RATES

And then began the swift-sequencing projections that would represent logical-mathematical operations so any alien could read them right.

In the hush I heard Fujiwara's blurry voice say, "So, thus any stone thrown . . ." But I was not to hear the philosophy of ripples. At that moment, the orderly transmission pattern on the screen fragmented into nothingness as if someone had stroked the tape with a magnet. The screen now read, in blurry, slightly slant, letters:

WE READ YOUR MESSAGE
PLEASE AWAIT OUR COMMUNICATION

The room silenced. One of the console intercoms buzzed. The technician who took it turned to Mummett and the navigation officer. You might have heard a pin drop, let alone his report.

"Sir, it's the standard audio-visual entry request."

"But," said the officer, "we locked our boards out of the ordinary station intercom system. No one can get through on those lines during transmission."

The technician waved his hand at the panel behind him. "Our comm panel shows that no phone internal to the station is asking entry. But the request is in our wires." There was a long pause.

"Could they do it from outside?" said Mummett. "From outside the station? From a distance?"

Several of the technicians huddled next to the consoles. I heard nothing clearly until one turned back to Mummett.

"Consensus is they have to know a lot more science than we do. I don't know who these people are. But anyone who says hello using means like this is someone you better say hello back to." The console intercom buzzed a second time.

"Turn 'em on," said Mummett.

And so Ambassador-Communicator Kagu snapped into electro-magnetic spectral view in the open center of the Comm Board room. We were all to call him Lord Langur. His lean, white-furred frame was human-tall, but his head still larger and his eyes, huge, brown, and whiteless. What struck one afterward was the ease with which he moved into our lives and concerns. And no wonder, I suppose. He had a graduate degree in a subject that from his appearance changed meaning. Anthropology. His English seemed to be derived more from watching Tarzan-and-the-Round-Table videos than from IBBC.

"It's all out there, you understand," said the Ambassador, his immense glittering eyes moving from one to another of us. (The technician stuttered over that, too. "He could see you, you know. They elicited structured backfeed from the room. God knows how they manage it.")

"It's all out there, you understand. All those early dreams of your cultures. Everything happens somewhere out there in our galaxy. The frolicking animals, the talking non-ape animals, of your folklore. Angels and devils, imps and sprites. All the possible, and unexpected or dreamed of, combinations of biology, and situation, neurological fiber and thinking program. It's all out there."

The Lord Langur bowed elegantly, swirling his purplish robe, to Go-Candy. "And we admire your variety, too. So happy to welcome you all." The bow folded robe and legs together, leaving a Buddha-like Ambassador a meter above the floor.

"Well my dears," said he, "I know you all will be thinking why haven't they phoned us before? And I am afraid—well I told myself I would have to tell you this and it is a sticky point—but the point is that you had not sent out anything in the past that we could consider a proper attempt at communication.

"Do you know," said Lord Langur, and suddenly something in his voice cooled the room until the hair stood up on the back of your neck, "do you know that we got a gold metal record from you a hundred and fifty of your solar rotations ago? Pompous and condescending guck. And then that little slab just before—an outline of human male and female, genitals uninformatively removed, your male standing before female, hand raised, female hands down at waist. Ho! as if you male humans were the message senders, females not saying hello, and as if your message to us were 'keep away from our women.'

"Hardly a promising start," said the Lord Langur, "but there it is. And the worst point is that a narrow portion of your intelligent population sends the message, while murdering, enslaving, torturing, other intelligence on Earth. Not representative, you understand. Hardly a sound basis for a dialogue. One responds to hello only from one who hellos with the full heart." And then the hair-raising cool left the room.

"But now your hello is certainly a hello." The Lord Langur bowed to Go-Candy, his lean, furry form curling, lithely, gently. "We are happy to hear hello from something like a fair spread of you. Happy to see you worked in someone whom the whirgers and the Bootes folk could be proud of. They're self-perpetuating metalloids, what you would call robots, I suppose. You shall have to be used to them.

"I must say I rather admire them. To build your children out of affection and rational choice and craftsmanship rather than, like us, driven by a primitive animal instinct, a genetic program as old as the genes themselves. To build your children—ah, that is something, or so Bootes folk tell one—they see our art as nothing more than a perverted substitute for our hopeless desire to build children. The whirgers split off from their mammaloid ancestors over twenty thousand of your years ago. Now they occupy twenty-odd planets and we have a few in my own home system. Mostly they hire out as what you might call technicians.

"And the Bootes robots? Well, it's hard to explain briefly. You might say that they began as a work of art and just got out of hand. Charming individualists, the Bootes folk, you understand. And a trifle naughty.

"Metalloids do, you understand, have a tendency to get tedious on the subject of evolution." Lord Langur winked at us. He made as if to doff his invisible hat to the consoles and screens. "Tedious. You understand that they naturally believe that mammaloids, if not chordates or hydro-carbon mechanisms in general, are a transitional episode in nature's evolution into robots and computers, into metalloids. 'The mammal is nature's way of producing the thinking organism per se, the metalloid.' That's the sort of thing they're always saying.

"Tedious, as I said, though not exactly easy to answer. Metal, and silicon, as they say, is the material of thought. You just need a slimy hydro-carbon intermediate stage to get to it. The whirgers in particular make rather a point of saying that a simple microchip can compute faster and more reliably than this mass of neurology." He tapped his head.

"As I said, tedious." The Lord Langur threw out his simian hands. "But, to be honest, they make the point that every civilized planet eventually gets multipurpose metalloids with the same basic logical circuitry and binary machine language. While the tailless simian, the ape, is actually not all that common."

The Lord Langur drew his hands in to grasp the

folds of his purplish robe. He caught my eye, his huge, brown, langur-proportioned eyes like pools in which I might comfortably sink. He bowed low and brought his robe up as he rose. His long, peach-fuzzed tail swung up behind, the tip smoothly curving up around his right side and in a forehead salute. Up tails all!

"You understand the PROCONGO premise is quite right of course," said the Lord Langur to the rest. "Hydro-carbon cellular life pops up all over. And it leads to bilateral organisms. Eventually, the high-powered, backboned and brained mammaloids. And partial bipedalism, grasping-fingered paws, large brain, and the whole shebang. But you are astonishingly nearsighted about tails.

"Mammals are, of course, naturally five-limbed, not four, naturally tailed. In arboreal environs it does its natural gripping, balancing job. Aquatic mammaloids use it as a flipper. Flatlanders use it for a variety of adaptations, as if it had lost its central purpose—balance in running and leaping, display, pest dispersal. When generalized mammals came down from their multidimensional arboreal environment, they came down in order to form a platform for big brains. A temporary compromise in which some mammaloids lost their natural fifth limb. We tend to think that they traded their multidimensional, their spacial, birth-right for a simpler chair design." He smiled at us and did a swirling flip, landing easily and slowly again on his back limbs. He was obviously in much less than Earth gravity.

"In space, in weightlessness and low gravity range,

251

mammaloids finally reestablish the conditions they are suited for, their destiny. We have a saying about thinking creatures with tails. 'A tongue in the world' for the tongue is the only single, nondual sense-motor organ aside from the tail, and the tongue is concealed. We belong in space, eh, Sally? We with tails, tales?'' Here our spokes-trinity, Go-Candy, broke into our mutual admiration society.

"You seem," she said, "to know a lot about the Oxford Study Group, and me and Sally and so on, and the whole PROCONGO project. How have you followed this so closely? How? Why?''

"Well''—here gave the Lord Langur his most engaging grin—''we've been filming it, you understand. Literally, taking pictures with a concealed camera so small you haven't detected it. Filming interesting events. We haven't interfered of course.''

"So you've made a video of us," I accused, "while not directly talking to us because, as you see it, we had not properly said hello, said it representing a range of Earthian intelligence. But isn't making videos of us interfering?'' I had a funny feeling about this.

"We anthropologists," said Lord Langur, "as do all students of uncivilized cultures, follow the rules. We don't interfere with, make ourselves known to, the savage thinking species we study. In this case our change arose innocently. We picked up some space junk, anthropoid artifacts, for examination and catalogue. A find, because while we can observe your behavior closely on Earth we couldn't take physical samples. Only we found a living human body, a

252

human body with prehensile tail, in the spacer work debris.

"Now we were in real trouble with our Primitive Subjects committee. So naturally we pulled out, putting things back the way they were, the best we could make of it. Shaped a path that would send a blank-brained but viable body into Earth orbit." The astrogators had said that Sally Cadmus had aimed her body unbelievably well.

Lord Langur coughed diffidently.

"Given the accidental, unintended nature of our contact with the Sally Cadmus body—your body, eh, Sally?—we bent the rules to put a humanly invisible instrument into the body to record what was going on around it. The camera is located in your tail tip, Sally. Your clothing often masked it. But we've got some good action shots."

"This is for anthropological studies; we are your field work?" I asked Lord Langur.

"Well, no, not quite. I must confess"—here his eyes grew gentle enough to engage the hardest soul in the room—"I must confess that we were also interested in the story, the drama of it all. The frizzie will be for popular distribution so to speak. I had proposed 'Tarzan and the Round Table' untranslated. But they insisted on a title that I could translate as 'The Tailless Savages' or 'Beyond Humanity.'"

"Of course you understand," added the Ambassador, "you understand that that's just my attempt to translate into English. Of course you understand that what I'm translating as 'humanity' is our word for us. And what I'm translating as 'savages' is our word

for you, whether of tailless or other Earth variety."
The Ambassador coughed. "I am sure it will display
your character fairly. I have written some Anthropologist's Notes to go with the Frames." He looked
around. "Warts and all is your expression, yes?"

Monkey shine.

THE BEST IN SCIENCE FICTION

Ben Bova

☐	53200-7	AS ON A DARKLING PLAIN	$2.95
	53201-5	Canada	$3.50
☐	53217-1	THE ASTRAL MIRROR	$2.95
	53218-X	Canada	$3.50
☐	53212-0	ESCAPE PLUS	$2.95
	53213-9	Canada	$3.50
☐	53221-X	GREMLINS GO HOME	$2.75
	53222-8	(with Gordon R. Dickson) Canada	$3.25
☐	53215-5	ORION	$3.50
	53216-3	Canada	$3.95
☐	53210-4	OUT OF THE SUN	$2.95
	53211-2	Canada	$3.50
☐	53223-6	PRIVATEERS	$3.50
	53224-4	Canada	$4.50
☐	53208-2	TEST OF FIRE	$2.95
	53209-0	Canada	$3.50

Buy them at your local bookstore or use this handy coupon:
Clip and mail this page with your order

TOR BOOKS—Reader Service Dept.
49 W. 24th Street, 9th Floor, New York, NY 10010

Please send me the book(s) I have checked above. I am enclosing
$_____ (please add $1.00 to cover postage and handling).
Send check or money order only—no cash or C.O.D.'s.

Mr./Mrs./Miss _____
Address _____
City _____ State/Zip _____
Please allow six weeks for delivery. Prices subject to change without
notice.